MUSE-ECHO BLUES

MUSE-ECHO

BLUES

XAM CARTIÉR

HARMONY BOOKS   NEW YORK

For my brace of Aces: Mary Carter Wilson, Kristin Wilson Hayes, Gregory Eiland Hodge, and the spirit of Albert Wayne Wilson—

For wordworker Eugene B. Redmond, poet Jayne Cortez, musicologist Horace E. Mansfield, Jr., and extraordinary-editor Mary Ellen O'Neill—

For poet Cornelius Eady and artist Sarah Micklem with their New York adlibility—

And for the spirit of virtuoso composer John Daniels Carter. *Resquiat in musica.*

Copyright © 1991 by Xam Cartiér

Published by Harmony Books, a division of
Crown Publishers, Inc.,
201 East 50th Street, New York, New York 10022.
Member of the Crown Publishing Group.
HARMONY and colophon are trademarks of Crown Publishers, Inc.

Manufactured in the United States of America

Library of Congress Cataloging-in-Publication Data
Cartiér, Xam Wilson.
Muse-echo blues : a novel / Xam Cartiér.
p. cm.
I. Title.
PS3553.A7843M87 1991
813'.54—dc20 90-48658
CIP

ISBN 0-517-57793-3

10 9 8 7 6 5 4 3 2 1

First Edition

If you are not a myth, whose reality are you?

—Sun Ra & His Omniverse Arkestra

Piano improvisation *Myself When I Am Real* (*Adagio Ma Non Troppo*)

Charles Mingus

MODE one

That Onyx Knack

~~~~~~~~~~~~~~~~~~~~~~

And Black Muzak

~~~~~~~~~~~~~~~~~~~~~~

At a cocktail party in a downtown complex—it's chock full of folks as far as the eye can see, in the atrium (where I'm on duty as guest) and up on peripheral floor overhead with Urban Professnulls poised at porticos that pockmark the balcony. Folks up there seem more laid back— See? There's a cleancut woman who's shoeless, her Picone kicks've been nudged to the side by her libertine toes, though that sort of thing's not to be found here in the mobscene below, where guttight light laughter laces the bootstrapper room.

Just dig this cast of uprising BUPs, women straight from pages of *Onyx;* all the men are *Mahogany Man*— As for me, dig the blackfokes' first clue, yep, my hairdo: it's sadly undone and lacks discreet glue of sheer Ultra Sheen— Just look at this hair on my head with nerve to be natural, picked into post-'fro compliance and stuffed through token barette so that long strands spray fountain-like forward, a takeover bush of cascading kinks in a milling milieu where co-guests are laid, sprayed, and ready to get paid; their 'do's are *down,* the sorors' at least—their coifs are all fried, dyed, and laid to the side.

Nate's the legit guest who's seen fit to lure me and squire me— "We'll meet there at four by the door," so he said. And just where in this limbo is he? Caught up in work or maybe just snared by his own Time of People of Color, sundial connection, caught by his own C.P.T.? I step forward to see and find myself in the judging arena, appraised on all sides by eyeshadowed eyes, disappointed: I've failed my charge to uplift the race by appearance, a woeful waste of raw possibility.

The set's full of BUPPIES and music of fusion, black muzak that girdles the scene with a no-challenge tease of lean saxophone keys squeezing a tune from the heart of the lower escarpment where a miniband's stationed to spout out sweet winecooler sound. Thin bass, snared traps, and set-in-ways sax—they seem to conspire just to mire me in drudge-music sludge. Yet there's hope in the form of a saving-grace vocalist, she being slim-pretty with doe-slant eyes and fullcurve lips kissing lyrics when she leans in to croon, *"You put your spell o-ver me. . . . You make me sat-tis-fie-yied. . . ."* Not bad afterall, this sooth-tune they're in process of weaving—it makes a simple weft but no matter; it's good sometimes when the warp is forgotten and all we require is a simplestitch songwrap for warmth and that's all. *Frisco Finesse* the group calls itself; I've heard them work up a lather on straight-to-it jazz at a newmusic venue called Koncepts, though right now's not time for that *avant garde* energy, not here in BUPPIE valhalla, this flash-n-dash showcase— Everyone knows BUPs don't dig jazz like their counterpart YUPs; BUPs dig their BMdub

Beamers, that's all. See how even this band's ignored and taken for granted as if they're a flipside of so much black wax? No one gets off on or gives themselves up to musicians or music: that's what disgusts me in subconscious key. Whoever heard of blackfokes at a blast where nobody so much as taps toes to the music, or gusts out a *"Yeah!"* or *"Uh-huh!"*? Well unprick your ears, cause all through the house not a creature is stirred. . . . In a word, we could be at the symphony lined up in row after row of conducted-cue minds untuned to improv and arch spontaneity, heedless of make-do to here-and-now cue, tastedeaf to what we cook up with our ingenuity. Just dig this stew of meltingpot lickers, they stick to the broth where it's spiceless, so *nice.* . . .

I'm chewing this through in my mind, breaking it down into bits mixed with rancory spit of *I've had it; I'll split!* when thought, it's arrested by peptic congestion of *What's this I hear?*— I can't help but eavesdrop two BUPmen nearby:

"I mean to say I got what I got under my *own* power, under my own steam." A stout man hiss-whispers the words with a shout's loaded clout. *"N*obody got for Hank, man, but Hank."

"I wouldn't say *that*, Hank—" a tall talker fires.

"I would," Hank shot back. "My curriculum vitae's as thick as your wrist. I went through school on my own—"

"By way of affirmative action, man," the interrupter interposed. He's brownish black and horn-rim glasseyed, with rectangular face full of furrows.

"Affirmative action didn't *keep* me in school." The

thickset man looked away with distaste then snapped his gaze back. "That's why they ought to *dump* those goddamn AA programs. They make for confusion, make it look like we don't measure up—"

"What are you saying?" The slim man is salty, as bitter as bark. "You used EOP as a stepping-stone, man. Civil Rights gains helped *you*—"

"I *told* you, Clyde, and you know it, Hank used *Hank* as a *black* stepping-stone. Now get to that and you keep it." He coughed up a chuckle. "That's just the problem. Whitefolks think we slid in under the gate—"

"Fuck what whitefolks think."

"Run that back? That's not what you say in your day-to-day business—"

"That's a whole other circus. You know it."

"It's the same ball of wax. The bottom line is, Can you hold up your end of the stick or not? Are you a go-getter or not? Can you cash out what you bring into a share of the market or not? Man, this life is capital inten-sive—"

"Birdshit if I ever heard it!"

"Wake up and face facts, man. You know what you are, Clyde?"

"You sound like a pet-nigger pawn. You should hear yourself."

"Know what you are? A hypocrite. A—"

The tall man's jacked aback. "Me? I'm the hypocrite? Man, I know *my* origin—"

"Know your place, you mean," says the broad three-pieced other. I face *up* to my roots!"

"They're wrapped around your neck. Any fool can see

that. *'You'll never get out of this life unblack.'* Du Bois told you that a long time ago. Read *The Souls of Black Folk*, circa 1903."

"What I'm trying to do is to stay in this life, brother. To stay in the game and stay sane."

"Yeah, well the other team's winning. Look at your scoreboard."

"The problem with you—"

"The problem with me is, I see through *you*."

"At least I'm for real." Words spouted from lips set in creases like vertical clefts in Hank's jawline. "You take what you can from your so-called 'community,' knowing full well those niggers that pad your pockets have little or nothing in common with *you*—"

"Black skin, man. You forget that?"

"The lowest common denominator. I'm not interested in that, and neither are you. You don't *live* with those niggers, Clyde; you choose *not* to *live* with those niggers. And why? Because you know you've got more in common with your neighbors in Miltonia, man, in white suburban high-toned Miltonia, where—"

"Man, I choose to live where I can *live*. You know the score; don't play greenie with me! Why should I put my family through everyday hell, Hank, like live in crack land . . . send my daughters to pimptime high schools—"

"No shit, Sherlock." The stout man broke out in a crossfire of laughs. "You can act like some kind of Man Of The People when you're with those lowlife clients of yours, forking out their pitiful pennies for pie-in-the-sky insurance they'll never get to see. . . . Be Kunta Kinte to *them*, Clyde. Don't run that jive up to me. I'm on to you, man. I see you in Miltonia with your high-yella wife—"

"Don't bring Megan into this, Hank."

"*You* brought her into it, Clyde. You brought her into that lifestyle of yours." He short-barked a chuckle. "At least I'm honest with myself about getting away from those rawrub ghetto niggers, man, those *dependent* pitiful niggers, latterday darkies; they're crude, they're rude, they're loud and *wrong*. I'll tell you straight from the gate: I fully intend to stay as far away from those worthless niggers as possible. I can't *get* as far away from them as I need to be!"

It's no news to me, the upshot of their words. . . . I feel like a wraith on the wing from haven to knell, circumspect-moving through sounds of opinion, unfiltered, pell-mell, e.g. from a He to a She and then She back to He:

"*. . . So what sign are you?*"

"*Pessimism. With bitterness rising.*"

Then from threepiece briefs to each other:

"*. . . and what's wrong with COOL?*"

"*Not a thing. If black folks weren't cool, we'd break out in a rash like nobody's seen. . . .*"

Then from two Fashion Fairies posed in tableau:

"*He flubbed Clue Number One, so I gave him Clue Two: Less Subtle. But he brushed on by that, so I took him to Clue Three: Forthright. . . .*"

"*Well that's 'cause he's slow to change. Lawyers don't believe in change til they can see the whites of its eyes.*"

And from mustachioed BizBUP to bearded companion:

*"Know what I did in management meeting when J.T.
tried to trip me?*

Laughed, right out loud. See, I'd already booked him
for one-way solo flight. . . ."

Then from overglossed raw-edged neo-BUPettes:

"She's Born Again now. Says that's the new her."

"Yeah, well, she best *to catch up with her old devilish
self. . . ."*

But the muzak is back, it rolls up *forté* after opening
bars of Jackie Mac's *Jacknife,* to which my mind turns on
its axis like a green plant to sun til I realize it's only a
warm-up while the saxist recalls he can *blow* if need be,
but not here where his fellow muse-makers already have
oozed into fusion, swirling us into a pool of poor flotsam,
musical oatmeal oozing through coustics like so much raw
glue. Yet in merciful no-time the band takes a break and
I'm freed from con/fusion! I think for a moment of seems-
liberation and sure nuff here comes a change of musical
fare, piped in through overhead stereo air although nobody
near seems to dig this or care— Over dialogue din I can
just make it out: soulful contralto, a diva's contralto, it's
Live From the Met! in mid-broadcast, radioed through on
a wild-art-type cue of its own. Leontyne! No doubt about
it, it's suave Leontyne who wears *savoir faire,* devil may
care for the rest of the fray; she came to play on the other
team's turf as visiting star from racial afar, but no matter,
she knows how to mow her way through those lone Euro
wetmisted modes for a few. *Yo,* Leontyne! Sow that ripe

soul into furrows of (Hark!) *Rigoletto;* you know it like I
do: soul makes for a fortified mulch. . . .

But don't let me elate when I oughta deflate with the
aid of jagged-edge truth: The world of expedience hates
what we mock-call "coincidence," so I oughta know to
expect a swift end to all joy that's unprogrammed to preplanned agenda. And what did I tell you? See what I mean?
No sooner's Price eased through the sound syst than someone unseen wrenches what must be a radio dial linked to
secrete discreet fill-in-blank music now wafting ahead in
'Tyne's stead, pudding-type music that lumps into clumps
in my head.

I retrace my steps in a fury this time— I'll find Nate,
say *Bye! Gotta glide!* and then fuck it, I'm went; I've served
my sentence, enough is e(nevermind)nough. Yet so much
for makeshift, instead of escaping I find that I'm penned
in by splendor, a wedge of goodtimers plumped up with
themselves; one's holding court in a stiff saginaw suit. Will
you look at this cadre of overstuffed UPs? Splendidy ruppie
and fiddledee ree, "Oh I'm *so* sorry," says BizBUP. "No,"
says BUPette, "no, no *please*, pardon *me!*" *Fie on these
follies*, I've said in my head when the claque cuts abruptly
away from a woman who seems on the verge of dropping
her drink; when she slips now and then she whoops! tips
the bowl of her plastic-stemmed glass— Dig, she's done
it again with a loose worm-shaped grin to herself.

In ensuing confusion and partyers' parting I manage
to march through the mob—I'm a drum majorette with her
own drumming rumbles: *I'll push past you fashionettes yet!*
At the side of the exit two women talk at each other top-
speed— I've looked back behind me but can't make out
Nate or a stand-in type friend so've decided to pose as

close to the door as I can, having stumbled offstage to premature cue. *Look, Ma, I'm scriptless and plotless and wearing a fuckedup costume. . . .* But wait, *I've got STYLE, so fuck fashion!* I yell in my mind, but clandestine protest, it brings me no peace. It's like this I'm thinking when two women dig me and nod with tight smiles, smiling *Let us get on with our biz. . . .*

"You ready for this?" says the first one ("I'm May")—She's chocolate-hued sharp in her gabardine suit, muted blue, nipped in and tucked at the waist.

"I'm nothin *but* ready," her friend says ("I'm René"), a Rubenesque woman of curve after curve, colored burnished brown-black so with sass-it-back verve. She looks at my sundress and opensling sandals then eyes my face boldly, searching for shame, but I bold-stare right back with *oeuvre d'No Thing* and it zings straight to target; a caliber bluff always does.

"You up for this?" she pitches to me with just-we-three incline of down-focused eyes. *Come closer,* she gestures. No doubt about it, she's just lit enough to be forthrightly friendly in what you could say is a sisterly way.

"All I'm sayin," says her talk partner May, "is I'm lookin for some support from a man, and it ain't about money, at least not alone. . . ."

René dropped down on May's words like rain on a roof. "You mean even a man who's non-black."

"I mean whoever can *hang*." May looked at me when she answered René.

We've struggled past glee when "I want you to know, I heard what you said," says a woman nearby us the moment we've surfaced for sanity. The speaker's a woman whose conflux of blond braids lanks into vision, they rope your attention the moment you see her: hazel-eyed blackfem with beige pallid skin as product of that salt-n-pepper shakedown perchance? I wonder right off the top, then think of myself with my mace-colored skin so can't help but consider what all the dark world knows: that half-white blacks are darker skinned than full-black blacks who hail from fair-skinned kin. Thus goes the motley enigma, a wildcard comment on color accordance, Demomyth's black&white color accordance as if there were such a thing as black race and white race here in this cauldron of color pot melt, even down South with its total pop of octoroons— Everyone there's an octoroon or at very least sixteenth-oroon, since misedge times gone slavishly by. *Oh say, can you see? She's such a merciless mixer, dear Demomyth is, with pale forefathers wrapped up in her dark-colored skirts—*

So this sister beside me, black Goldilocks in her Pier 1 gown low-cut to reveal Surprise! freckled chest, with all that colorlessness going against her, to counteract seeming whiteness (and consequent lightness onstage when with blacks) she takes special care to talk overly blackly saying, "I woe/ncha tuh know. . . ." Her speech hangs heavy with its load of rough vowels, tough enough to stand on their own without need of a lean-to trellis type "*t.*" It seems to me that she makes her speech doubledip black in extreme, almost but not quite like a white who wants to play black for a few.

"It's your choice, you got the say. But if you wanna play, you gotta pay." Goldie's proceeding to rap, she goes on in this way for an onflowing while til she digs our chagrin at her butt-in, then takes time to blacktrack into *How are you? You all right?* entry to shadowy psyches of dark folks unknown. So "Well, sisterloves," she repaves her rough mode with passworded code, "pardon my rush. Yall caught my ear an it seemed we might be on the one."

We've adjusted with ease to her now *if-you-please* blunted tack, so "Hi, I'm me. Call me Kat," I say, leaning in toward new comrade. "And here's May. May, and René."

"Call me Chloe." She nods and handshakes our hands all manicured but for mine, because mine are mere tools to be used at piano, pianist's probes with prehensile nails cut square and foreshortened, the better to grasp onto cues from the muse. I note that Chloe's too are jagged-art stubbed and seem to be rubbed here and there with some sort of taint, maybe acrylic or could be oil paint.

But enough of our curtsying courtesyed how do we do— "All I was saying," May recaps, "is I reserve the right to take care of *me.*"

"With whoever you please," says René. "It's your option, you're saying."

"And your optee just might be white." I push this in then rush out to where I should be, at the unseen edge of barbed repartee.

"The brothers, *they* dig the chance to choose white," proffers May.

René's in high lockstep with sistergirl May. "They tell me that white keeps em from bein uptight, say it keeps em loose."

"Yeah?" I jab in. "Well what's good for the gander is *down* for the goose."

I'd laughed it out and reaped a harvest of howls so severe that Nate gets the spirit to beat it on back from his war at the wine and food bar— Nate, fine as wine, tall and divine, six feet four *fresh*—Do you hear me? BUP or no BUP, with his walk to one side slightly stooped from the weight of his up-attaché. . . . Do-or-die Nate dressed in charcoal three-piece for the occasion or maybe en route from his office, Nate dappered down with big smile as usual, hair cut in boxcut squared off at edges that balance his angular jaw jutting forward— It's our laughter that's called him, *carefree blacklaughter free from weird strife*, he must think in the same way a tourist white would, yet it's then when Nate's hurried forward flashing his grin that Chloe's confiding, "Jus' let it be *us* wit' that whiteboy tho. Don't you know to the bloods we'd be 'sellouts,' ya see."

The three of us can't help but break up again when "Now wait just a minute," Nate makes himself say, looking behind him as if for his troops, which he finds in the form of a tall lanky man loping toward us who seems to be drawn to our forcefield by Nate's vibrant need. The newcomer strides forward with taut regularity, he being mid-brown-skinned with insight-full eyes piercing through what could be fierce disapproval.

"They got you hemmed in, bruh?" he flash-smiles to Nate.

"No thing, Chet," Nate tells him, "I'm holding my own." They chuckle: *No jive!* and slap manly five.

But Chloe's intent; she's bent on agenda that only she knows. "When it's a sistuh with her white dude, to hear the brothuhs tell it, it's got to be that old slave-rape theme an nothin else."

"Replay *Mandingo*." I can't help but prance in and dance out again.

"What took you off on *this* bent?" Nate tysons in, looking at me then at dormant response from his erstwily partner, newcomer Chet. Nate seems to be thinking,

*All right, if it's all up to me, I just might mike-tyson
again. . . .*

"Dig on this," Chloe goes on, but then's when a
darker-skinned woman joins in—she's chunky and rouged
and geared up in *gucci* galore, a black successette who, it
seems to me, is tanked past control so that she's pulled
past the usual BUPPIEnorm stops.

"If you don't mind," Sisternew laughs long and
strong—yep, she's running on Full—"I'd like to share
something that happened to *me*."

"Go right ahead," Chet says with expansive mien and
demeanor, winking cleanly at Nate, seeming to indicate
Whatever it is, we can deal, *do ya dig?* And Nate raises
eyebrows at Chet: *You're right with* that. . . .

"I was walking down the street with a white friend of
mine, a real quiet guy, and here come these black so-
called brothers sidling up to us—"

Chet cut her off. "Why we got to be *'sidling'?*"

Nate checked with Chet. "And why have we got to
be *'we'?*"

Three quarternote beats then a series of rests worked
their way through what had turned into blues in this measure during which Newsister seemed to be musing. I noted
her struggle for *center*, saw her strain to bring herself back
around; she'd be self-contained if at all she could help it;
it's why she'd invested in formalized speech due to mustbe
discomfort with deepblack appearance in her workaday
world of light white. "As you like," she was saying. "Black
men walked up to us, men on the street, examining us
from head to toe—"

"So?" Chet let us know. "They didn't like what they
saw."

(*Who the hell does?* came the thought thick as thugs. It must've been fueled by mass energy. . . .)

"And, and get this." SN was heedless of happenstance hurdles. "Two of them had nerve enough to come right up and comment—"

"Black folks are outspoken," Chet said with a shrug. "We're an expressive race of people."

Nate thought it through in a twink. "Now *that's* true."

" 'What you *do*in wit dis grey boy?!' one of these loudmouths had nerve enough to ask me right there on the street—"

Chet gave her his rue as fast-wasting patience. "You had a problem with that?"

"But wait," New insists. "There's no way any of you have the right to run herd on me!"

"There goes that 'we.' " Nate winks at me. "Now let's see. There's the Brute, the Clown, the Fop, and the Stud—"

"That's us all right," Chet pitched in. "All four divisions of blackmen."

"Satanized or sanitized," I stagewhisper and blister thin skin as if I'm a sun armed with ultra-v light. "Well, hell, look at us." I point to the wimmin. "Mammied, bewhored. . . ."

"I'll tell the world"—Sisternew now's looking ready to fire— "That whiteman of mine was the first man to be supportive of me in what I wanted to do, and"—she fired into the lull—"he didn't feel a *threat* about it."

"Why would he?" Nate capped. "He knew he was there to fill in your blank."

Our faction was fractured; all of us broke up or down in ridiculous glee. We'd attracted auxiliary critics and

listeners so that our claque was now full of dissidents, die-
hards, and renegade BUPs, among them a guy who called
out, "You sure know how to simplify!"

"Well never you mind now," Nate jawed back, "it's
never too late to complicate!"

It's in follow-up mayhem of mirth and new joiners to
clique (Let *us* into this new in-crowd groove!) that the pop
band returns/pops up on the stand and I'm urging a surge
through the centerstage sax, a wild tenor scream fired from
spiritful throat, something to boost us away from homebase
so we gain new perspective, which's what good jazz does,
it launches our vision by way of our ears— And for a
moment it seems that the saxist is serious, he's laid down
a few bricks of be-bop type blasts, maybe paving the way
from lush past to plush future of rounded, ripe, challenging
notes full of creative hope, say on the order of Odean Pope's
whirlwindfull sound with clean *hold-it!* bold wheeeyop
stops on a dime. Pope's *Saxophone Shop* is the miraculous
earful that eases to mind as a contrasting tease/I mean
please feed me some muse-ic of nutrient energy, serve me
some vibrant vitality, dish me up nourishing forwardwing
thrust!

"What's on your mind?" Nate hugs me to him and
sidesteps away from the fray. "You see, all caught up in
thought." He's kissing my temple, letting lips linger a
moment. I break out in laughs—now why'd I do that? I
disavow me when I mince ultra-femininely or wince from
sheer overstirred nerves. Nate's unalarmed at my show of
distress though—but then he's used to juggling confusion,
Nate of bright eyes with slight slant so he looks to be always

in scrutiny, sizing up situations, appraising— I resee him making his way through pockets of people, caught for a moment in greetings of friends that he passes, heading toward me from far overseas of this set.

"Kat, let me run something by you . . . see what you think." His eyes focus briefly on distance, sight slipping out for a few then back in.

"Go right ahead; I'm all ears." (Or damn near. . . .)

"It's the gig. . . . A *particular* trip at the gig. . . ."

I can't help but note how he looks prime, disconcerted or no he's still debonair with his musing lips pursed to one side so that steep afro-indio cheekbones jut forth. Just dig his squaregrip hands steady though ready, not nervous— I gotta admit, I'm a fool for élan; my penchant goes clear back to . . . when? Some folks can't help it / exude capability/seem to demand, *Hey world, lean on me!* Nate's sign is Libra; he struggles like hell on the scale of good balance to be.

"There's this guy at the circus," Nate confronts my distended attention.

"At Townsend Behemoth?" I picture that corp in a complex that's set on Wall Street of the West, a skyscraper looming in cashflow of clouds. Below at serf level of corporate turf are workaday zombies coughed up from the subway: men striding surefooted in sensible shoes; women from pages of *New Self* and *Savvy*, killer-bee dressed and glossed for success. . . .

"You know how it goes. There's five of us there as you know, one per division—one in data design, one in sales and service, one in customer relations, one in public affairs, and me. I'm the personnel chip."

"There's a few more though, right? A receptionist—that cold freeze-dried sister I met the day we did lunch—"

"Oh sure, we've got chocolate chips throughout the whole cookie. I'm talking management though."

"Oh I dig," I jibe quickly, wishing he'd deepdive on down straight into the issue; my last hope of sanity's calling from outside in free pure night air of amazing escape. . . .

"It's this . . . *brother*, I guess you could call him." Nate flinches and says it, presenting a visage of choking down hell-flavored medicine stewbrewed by haints. "This joker—name's Jake—he's been fucking up lately; he's late on the job, sometimes he's high . . . though who the fuck isn't? You gotta do *some*thing. We all do a dab. Even the manager hoovers nose-candy, and all the veepees, hell, they *live* in the men's room with burners and flasks—You should see it on overtime nights!"

"It must look like a vigil of champ Campfire Boys."

C'est la vie blanc. . . . We laugh to each other at protocol scams that always seem to encircle just us, the dark few in a white-sinner legion of bold whooping sin.

"And your buddy?" I downsimmer to say.

Nate gives me his look of grinless chagrin. "Jake's in no position to dope on the job. What's more, he *looks* high. Looks and acts like Dr. Spock. Sounds like him too, especially by noon."

"He must be into a time-release high."

"Slides through the halls with his eyes at half-mast. . . . Gives gaff to his supervisor—his boss is a 'neck, wouldn't you know it, a cornfed cracker from Georgia."

A ripple rises up in me; I mash it down and just focus on Nate quick-swigging getaway drops of his drink.

Nate shakes his head. "Blood's always looked down on me—"

"Looked down on *you?*"

"Regards me as an Oreo and doesn't mind letting me know it. Thinks I'm in league with the greyboys, tomming in some sort of slick way. Imagines I'm secretly shining their shoes. . . ."

"What brought that on?"

"You be the one to tell me. He seems to think to be beautifully black I should cover for him."

The muzak rolled up, it cut Nate no slack with its shallownote furrows crimping our mindset to devilish rote. He deft-rubbed the wrinks of his forehead. "I'll catch you next week," he said with his rain-or-shine grin. "When I'm back from recruitment outreach we'll get together. I'll fill you in on developments then."

He soft-pressed a kiss on my temple, letting his lips languish at rest before he took flight. Then next thing I knew he was gone like a light, making me mull, *Was it something I said or should've fed back?* I masticate this for a moment, munching it down to a paste in my mind until *Fuck it,* I think with Nate's same fedupness— Wasn't I aimed for the door and its open port promise? I've got a date with myself, so later for Nate— To thine own shadow be true!

Lindy Hop &

Non-Stop Bop

To thine own shadow. . . . It's no sooner than I'm out and alone on my own that musing takes over my consciousness; I've just seated myself in a bistro named Waterloo West near the scene of said party, when insistent vision sudden-wafts in, seeming so far to be only a daydream, a harmless mere series of scenes of the sort that artists are all spacecase prey to/or so I told me back then at the onset, then when they'd only begun. I heard her voice then at the start of the story, "she" being the narrator and also the star of a sequence of strange escapades; doings caught up in time's coil to the past, exploits about which I knew nothing back then.

"*Memories, old memoirs,*" she began. I have some of my own from the forties, though I don't look for form among memories— How can I say this? I'm not sure they add up or piece together, yet they oughta be sifted through—

accounted for. Like the time I first met Chicago there in K.C., when all thru this land the watchword was *band* . . . when D.C. had Duke E, K.C. had McShann, Memphis had Lunceford, Baltimore had Chick Webb, New York had Fletch Henderson plus a lot more ado, St. Lou had The Missourians, an Chi had Luis Russell, Lou Armstrong, an the first few big bands to come thru.

'Go was steppin up to the stand, this man lookin like a walkin desert, dry, tan, with a sun-warmin smile, had his head cocked to one side like he owned a world he brought with him. . . . " 'Go!" went the whisper thru the ranks of the regs & I could read ready grins of *Here we go!* all through the joint, starting from the stand. Slim & Slam were workin the stew out of a tapdance up there on the stage:

The flat-foot floogie wit the floy-floy—

They had us boppin, no stoppin straight down the aisles— *Look* out; I'm comin thru! Forefingers waggin— the guy next to me an his chick pulled off a series of serious flips; he'd stop to split an slide up every once in a while. Be-bop hoppin—the ballroom went wild, you couldn't help but jump on the floor an cut a raggedy rug with all your might—I pulled out all the stops with the first fella to find me. Wham! Whee-bop sha boop bam— we boogied forward, deadbeat back, broke out in the break- down an shimmied to the left— Man we couldn't help but go for broke. Then came 'Go through the madness, stridin clean an tall, a head above the best of em. He looked at me in my antics an winked a broad smile for a while that snatched me right out of the rhythm. I can see me now with my headband plume all bent outa shape, how I must've looked; I'd started straightenin myself up by reflex to please, pattin spit curls down near my ears, feelin the top of my croguinoled head for my rhinestoney crown, which I found to be cocked ace-deuce as usual— I ran my hands down the seams of my gown, straightened the hip sash in back— Then, bloomp diddely *boomp* came the tail of the tune leadin into the head of the follow-up jam, a cool slowdrag bluesy wrap-em-up number which 'Go brought in with a wail. Whatever the riff 'Go rode it with a loping swing that arced out wide an then closed in, eyes closed— The *sound* of the man, it oozed right into your soul, made you rack back all the sad undertones of a life fulla doub-ledge color— I sank down into a breezy sea of endless possibility til 'Go was thru and next thing I knew, he'd plowed thru the crowd an stood there smack-dab at my table.

"How you feel?"

"Almost cured," I shot back, an he couldn't help but laugh—"Tell you what," he jumped in. "There's more where that come from. You should hear me solo—"

"Thought I just did." I broke right in on his line.

"No jive, that's a fact. I got some special notes you need to hear."

"I'll just bet."

"We oughta get together. Take it from me."

"Nothin doin."

"What you doin by yourself, a sweet little dish that's as with it as you?"

"Lighten up now, don't try to softpedal me."

"If you don't come with me, I'll be awful sore."

"You'll bounce back. You got a strong constitution."

"You know, you're a hard chick to talk up on."

"That's the idea."

"You treat me like I'm up to no good. All I'm doin is makin the most of good opportunity—I'm not tryin to get you to hop in the rack."

"You just tryin to tantalize me."

"Take it from me."

"I hear you talkin."

"Why you want to *be* that way?" Despite himself, he started to grin. He'd even begun to pull out a chair for himself when—

" *'Go! Man, you comin or stayin?*" a baritone voice called out from the door.

'Go took a step an looked back at me. "All right, Sugar, if you miss your chance now, don't come bawlin an cryin to me."

I was put out. "I'll manage to live."

He pulled the chair out and sat down on its edge, leanin forward to whisper an make his words heard. "I want you to come with me," he said, lookin straight into my dance-away eyes. "*All* of us ain't fulla stuff, now. Some-a us cats are all right."

"Since when?" I countered. He'd hit the nail dead on the head.

"*Man, the ride's waitin. We gotta get in the wind!*"

"Hold onto your hat! My baby's got to get her wrap!"

I took my time to look sideways at 'Go who was all stirred up beyond cool. "Now that's a neat switch." Frenzy regardless, I settled back into my seat.

"STEP on it, 'Go!"

"Don't be like that now!" His voice'd grown out&
out urgent. *"In a minute!"* 'Go shouted an swiveled
to me. "See what you doin to me? Don't put me on the
spot."

"You won't be there for long."

"Sez who?" He gave me a thin winsome grin. "All
right then. I can't win for losin." He stood up now, snatchin
his coat. He kissed me on the cheek an picked up his horn
case. "I don't blame you," he said, "you gotta watch out
for cats talkin trash. A woman like you must *live* on the
lookout." He started to step, but stopped short an shook
his head. "I want you to know though, just for the record—
I'm no flim-flam, an I don't scam." He turned toward the
door an started to stride. I could hear him whistle some
riffs as he went, an the words to the tune took form in my
mind. *"You musta been a beautiful bay-bee, cuz BABY just
look at you now!"*

Top *that*. Now here's a dude who's willin to go for
broke an to knock himself out for what he believes in. How
do I know? Cuz I knew I was sore that that wasn't me—
I know my own score: I'm one cautious baby!

My own head broke in on my thoughts. *You might
ought to lay down your sword an your shield.*

Ain't that a blip? Yet I had to listen. Why shouldn't
I just shoot the works? For as long as I can look on, my
lovelife's been nowhere or near there.

Wise up, pal, said my head. *There's such a thing as
OVERDOSE cool!*

Oh, I dig. A fool an her cool are soon parted. Live a
little! This could be just the ticket. I'd started to grin to

my hope-happy self— I'm a quick study; it don't take me long to size up the sitch.

"'Go! Wait for me!" I heard myself call.

He stopped on a dime in 4/4 march time an his whistle slid into a looooony-tune note. He held out his arm just for me.

A One-Night Stand

With The Boys

In The Band

I . . . didn't know . . . what time it was
Life was no prize . . .
I want-ted love and here it was . . .
Shine-ning
out
of your eyes . . .

KITTY
Kansas City, 1945

I remember the time 'Go first came to see me, that
first Xmas Eve two years ago when he'd found himself left
behind in the war and it figured—there was no room at
the front for cats with orange piss-test returns, even in the
KP arena where most of his colored buddies were bound.
His 4-F got to 'Go, he let it get him down. Course when
I'm down I'm just like 'Go too, I keep to myself— Why

should I drag the next fool with my blues? Why is it that folks like to believe that love licks the blues, that it picks people up in testy hard times? I recall a fella knocking himself out to convince me that romance would help me / not hinder in handlin sharp-edge personal matters—he was scufflin to persuade me that a hookup with him would just fill the blank in my bill. I don't know about that, but sure as I'm Kitty, I do know this here: If you gotta hardsell somebody to love you, take it from me, love's doomed from the gate. It won't *place* an *likely* won't show, cause it takes two to tango in madness or love, whichever word you prefer. If you gotta run *game* on your lover to be, it's all over but the moanin, believe you me—romance is already dead on one side, and after death there's hell to pay by way of your own sadsack savings, highwater hell, it'll be up on you in no time, in the shake of a feeble fool's tale. If only I'd known! I can still see me now, when I'd barely hitched to K.C. from the sticks just to be the hatcheck girl that I claimed then as me. . . .

I'm crimpin my hair at the mirror in that redbrick flat where I live, got my waves bent just so in a glossy black river flowin upswept over one sand-colored ear, s-curl bangs dipped over left brow. I test-shake my head; nothin gives, so my slick marcel, it's neet and all-reet. . . . I spit into my cake of mascara and brush it on so that my lashes spike in dark sun rays round my eyes cuz 'Go seems to go for my eyes of surprise, then I spread a juicy plump bow of Certainly Red on my lips, add a dot to cheek dimple beside, and dust on a light veil of silk-smoothy powder, Nut Brown's the color—can't help what they call it; it works like a charm, coppers my skin to a shiny tan glow—and then uh-oh, say Ho! I ease into open-toe mules of ribbon-grain satin, hot scarlet—Well what do you know, I go for these strides, sharp new kicks. . . . *Well get to it then, let's go head an break em on in!* I can't help but take me some time out to dance. *Shop be oop bop be oop bay:* Mr. B's on my RCA Victor, he's blowin the brass outa "I Love a Rhythm and a Riff," workin the tune for all that it's worth, layin his horn down and loosnin his croon when it seems to be time to just bop past the stops. I've pranced to the chifforobe, dancing like a shoeshine boy, I *geche* to the sofa and *turkey* on back, *sconch* to the bureau, *mess-around* for a few, and then do a deft *skate* to the left. I'm thinkin of 'Go on his way all while I'm boppin, poppin my fingers. . . .

All on a sudden I gotta stop to beat time with a straw on the table—seems like I'm always workin the syncopate-theme of the sound into which or whatever surface I find, I soft-sucked my breath in time to the notes thinkin in rhythm, I gotta admit it, I love the man's style! An he does style awhile with that lightnin flash beam of his smile. In the darkest corner of the room I fancy his smile, it twinkles an winks straight at me—I see 'Go in front profile with that let-me-in gap between his teeth that I can't help but make like I taste with the tip of my tongue. Tan-haired, tan-eyed Chicago—When he plays Eckstine's band chicks don't know *where* to look, wish for extra eyes, one pair to train on Mr. B with his lick-it-up baritone lilt, the other to focus on 'Go an his hoarse bedroom horn, tall auburn 'Go born with those Houdini hands, square supple palms an lean magic fingers up to no good / all the good in the world when they wrap up my hand in their box of *home safe* for a while— I'll take that while though, let it be *said!*

"Stick with me, kiddo." 'Go pats Kit's thigh.
"Where'm I goin? I'm down for the count."
"Get a loada you." Unbuttons her midi-blouse.
Squeezes his lips in to cupsuck one currant of nipple.
"Don't go NO/where." His eyes are slight-closed . . .
he lies on his back telling her this:
*"When I wake up on the other side of the rainbow, I
want the first sight I see to be you."*

'Go'll be here soon— Where's my gown? It's *too*
down—deep bronzy pink done in layered chiffon so it drifts
with life of its own, moves in waves, it grooves to the pulse
in the calves of my legs. I'm here to tell you, this frock is
it, made of fabric so fine that it flows with suggestion and
brushes its tune on the sense-happy beat of my skin. Say
hey *hey.* . . .

I'm caught in mid riff at a high note of hope when I
hear 'Go's ride roll up to the curb down below, then there's
his key in the lock, yes indeed— The man seems to move
on his own crest of speed.

"Hey, tenor lady," he says, steppin in in his gladrags
of wide-slide lapels with his Staceys shined up to a mean
high-noon gleam. His eyes size me up in my glory, then
comes his kiss: "I missed you," he says with his fingers
playing the curve of my face. He bends me a raised rueful
eyebrow, inquisitive grin.

"Look what I made you for Christmas." He's un-
wrapping pages he's covered with brownpaper wrap against
snow that was drifting outside, a slight-seeming tease of
our weather to come. "You ready for this?" And he broke
into fuzzy up-tempo song, sounding nearlike he sounds on
his sax—"I wrote this for you." "In Feline Time," he'd

named the tune with its rash angle beat, explaining to me, "You ever dig *cats*, how they move? They flex like a coil, spring from a standstill that's like . . . you with me?"—he took time to kiss me—"like a *rest*. From a full-note rest into *Abracadabra!*: whatever dancestep will help em to *deal*, then back to inertia, a half stop this time, always alert, spiffy rippy, you dig? They're always all set to do whatever they need to, to deflect any upcoming damage, you dig. . . ."

I had one hand on my hip and my head, it was cocked in the know. "These must be colored cats. Am I wrong?"

"Baby, you know it like I do: *All* cats is colored. That's why we move like we do."

"No doubt about it." We fell out with laughs for a few.

I've noted how 'Go's takin stock of the room, its rose-patterned wallpapered walls with their brown and cream daguerreotypes, the new-painted radiator with its tray of my plants along its steamy length, the phonograph stabled in chifforobe drawer I had special-drilled so the cord wouldn't show, the mahogany cocktail table near the divan with its white-doilyed arms and slope back . . . and me as Queen Bee in my round-bottomed lowboy, me sittin poised as cool as can be, watchin 'Go go for me and my backdrop. Does he say so though? Nothin doin, he just goes on to kid me with, "Doll, you do snazz up these sorry surrounds." Leans down to me, nip-licks the lobe of my ear so I shiver and smile til I edge myself back into place: *Just be cool!*

No man snaps and I jump—I'm a woman full grown, not a new-dewed kid fulla trust and surprise. Not that I'm covered with crust, it's just time to get wise, so I'm prone to play close to the chest, to *cover* as much as can be.

'Go's laugh plays right past me though. . . . Look at
the fool fake a bent-waisted bow til I go on an give up a
grin.

"Dig how the lady doth balk," he says then. "Methinks
she intendeth to give me the slip, but gallant that I am, I
never say no to a challenge."

"Now whether you triumph, that all depends." I
quick-nab a minute to fathom the mystery depth in his
eyes, but I find myself sunk like Sam Spade when he's
new to the case, so I let 'Go take hold of my arm, snatch
my fur on the way out the door.

When we step in the club, all I can see is dappered-
down regulars, war-end high-timers, an jokers alike ragged
to the *nth*—there's gloss everywhere bounced off of shiny
high heels an florsheims an hair. Up near the stage are
ranks of musicians all sportin cool but achin to jam, includin some bopcats who're new so'll need to be judged
by their sound. Fact is though, I'll put it like this: If they're
here to blow with 'Go at his level, they're hip until time
proves em square. . . . Grouped at the front are the dues-
paid brass of the tunester ranks; they're jivin with each
other, signifyin, cuttin the dozens: *Hey is that you, pal?
I thought you was dead!" ("Man, I'm more alive than you'll
ever be!")* But hold it right there, hold onto your hat,
Jacquet's just soared into a solo, trailin lanky long trills
of high-register honks that loop through the air (Say *what?*
Is you nowhere?) like so many multi-toned streamers. I
latch onto one note and float to remote uncharted stars til
sixth sense, it grounds me for my own good. *"Just dig,
looka there,"* says my own head, and I dig what I could
do without for the rest of my days in this life: the sight of

shameless Mamie Flowers, that hellbent canary who chirps with the band, she's stalked up to 'Go damnear fore we squeeze into the door an heads turn to watch her travel through the throng—they know she's up to somethin of slithery interest, no good. While I was away in the music, Mamie's made up her mind to rush up an mash a fat kiss on 'Go's cheek. Get a loada her nerve—already she's pressed up against him like she's helpless-pushed by the force of the crowd. "Scuze *me*," she says to a dude groovin past who's caught off his innocent-bystander guard: *What's with this chick?*

Just take a look at this jinx . . . here she comes up to me with her sweet briny smile. Dig how her rhiney pale skin lights up with costumey glee. "Oh 'Go, who's your girlfriend? This your new heartthrob?" She squeezes my hand, overdoes it. "Well Angel, welcome to heaven! Don't mind my bad manners, I didn't see you!"

If nerve was cash, she'd be rollin in dough. "I didn't see the sky when I looked up today": I go on an say it, dish it straight to her, can't help but serve her a neat dose of dozens til 'Go drops his grin at dame Mamie long enough to nudge me with his elbow an I get the point though I can't help but think, *Well you do have to jam with the thrush, but for cryin out loud, I don't owe her a note.* I'll be the first to fess it: I've never been able to tone down my turn for sharp thrust an cut, while trickchicks like Mamie are sent to the planet with sawtooth natural skill— they come here with raggedy brass that's sassy enough to bring down an oak from the rear. Didn't see me like hell, well do tell—she spotted me *first* in her scam to get next to 'Go doncha know—*First, scout your position:* I'm wise to the el of surprise, I *know* how the battle strat goes an know when to fall back an regroup. What's this new non-sense now though? 'Go's whispered somethin to Mamie that makes her break out in a grin, then when she sees me scopin em both she lets out a loud cooked-up laugh that I need like somebody to bleed me. I've had enough of this tired twobit scene, it's draggin me out-an-out *down* when "*Just play it slow an hip-easy,*" my levelhead self says to me; "*Don't fool around an blow your top, you lose good ground that way.*"

"Hey, Kitty!" a voice shouts from the front of the room, and squintin I make out Jacquet—Jack's crookin a cue for me to run join him near the bandstand, which I do right away, slippin my arm from 'Go's grip with an all's-well pat: Now you get to that!— I give him my smile as I move to get hat. Let him glean my direction, he's a smart boy. . . . See? He hips up in no time, just like I knew that he would.

"Wait just a sec," he's sayin to Mamie, cuttin her off midseam in her gab. "Hold up, Kitty," he calls to my back, but I'm off & runnin/only stop for red lights, so I turn for a moment to bend him a wink, see him scuffle to peel off Mamie's fast clutch, see his smile turn to strain an snap back in place as I go right ahead to grab me some space and baby oh baby I'm *gone.* Now this is more like it. . . . I'm meetin a million cats as I pass thru the place. Wonders won't quit; up comes Sonny Stitt. . . . "Come on Kitty, knock me a kiss," he says with a grin back at 'Go still hemmed at the door. Stitt's tellin me bout Count Basie's band—sez he prefs it to Eckstine's cuz-a what Sonny calls Count B's "stretch potential."

"See," Stitt sez to me, "though Eckstine's got the young cats, so he's got a wellspring of the juice of what's

happnin now an better, what *will be*—I'm talkin that New
Thing they call it, that *Bop*." Stitt whispers this last an
then grins down at me. It'd be soon when he'd rush up an
say to me, "Hey! I'm off to the Apple to dig this cat *Bird*"—
he'd say the word with a catch like he knew Bird would
say one fine day talkin to Stitt with no stuff caught up in
it—"Man, I'm not long for this life. You carry on. I'm
leaving you the keys to the kingdom." Not knowing this
now though, Stitt's all aflit with his thought of "though
Eckstine *swings* now, don't take me wrong, Bill Basie lets
his cats *stretch*."

"In solo, you mean."

"Kitty, my girl, you' right on the dime— Keep it up,
you'll be hip in no time!"

"Go head, Sonny, make yourself happy, knock yourself out, go on, slander me."

He gives me his laugh. "I know what you know an
you know it like me: Count B lets his cats roam far an
wide, an that's how we *grow*, while him an the whole band
just pockmark our melody, see."

For a minute I heard Basie's tide of gushed chords,
then I made out his horn section takin a unified stand,
united in states a their rhythm an harmony. There they
were for a flash in a open-roofed room in the night of my
mind, one solid entity sittin then standin with clarinets,
saxes an other brass axes held upright then raised overhead
now held level, next lowered down an soundin right low
as they're lowered—the trombones an trumpets sound
blues-to-you mean as they lean to one side then the other,
one balanced body connected. They're showin the show-
manship Lunceford's band showed, with their horns as a
unit all lifted aloft, an their charts are as tight as the ones

Sunny Blount worked for Fletch Henderson's group. But the Count's band, it's workin blues through into goldennote jazz by way of spare quotes here an there next to soloists' highflown free melody, all of it spark-echo trimmified lean.

No sooner's Stitt split though than dig if you dare, here comes Prez Lester Young with that lean gleanin bop-walk dippin down toward me just bent to surmise my intent an to wise me in how he's got eyes just for me—that's what I see when he tips his porkpie hat smoothly; his movement is wrought in solid-caught rhythm, his every motion is taut as a drum. Prez stood the big bands on their saxophone ends—his praxis made sax the headline band ax. 'Thout him the sax was a horn like em all, made to be played like a trumpet they thought, Pops Armstrong's trumpet to be precise: Satchmo's sassy voice harddrivin brass.

"Hey, Mr. Mean Sax!" I wag back to his "Kitty!" showin how I'm in mind to cut him no slack. "That was some sweetness you served us up there." I nod toward the bandstand he's left. "You *death* on a beat." Some relentless riffs roll to mind: for a minute I hear me an earful of Prez an his ace Ladyday, them ridin the air beat for beat blowin sweetnasty blues straight outa the box, vocal to shadowphone, partners in Congo Square Old Orleans crime.

"See, Lady an me," Prez goes on to tell me, "we've got some new voodoo this sphere's yet to hear." An he must mean it too cuz I feel it already inside me, that black-an-blue rhythm Prez won't let rest, an neither will Lady—they keep the bands nappy an true.

I'll pull his coat to my thrill. "Prez, you all over them high notes! Just like a alto."

He gathers his looseness of suit coat around him. "If
you want it like a tenor I can play it like that too. You
see that's where the people get fucked at, you dig? I get
all kinds of insults about it." He mock-whines the rest.
"'You don't play it like you played when you were with
Count Basie. . . . ' I'm a man getting older and things, and
I got to look for young things, so I say, 'No! I don't remember no shit with Count Basie, you know, unless I have
eyes.' I've developed my saxophone and I play it, make it
sound like that alto, make it sound like a tenor, make it
sound like a *bass* and everything, and I'm not through
working at it *yet*. That's the way folks all get trapped up.
They go, 'Goddamn, I've never heard any player like this!'
That's the way I *want* things, that's *modern*, you dig? In
my mind, the way I play, I try not to be a repeater-pencil,
you dig? I'm always loosening spaces, laying out, or something like that. Don't catch me like that, Kitty. I'm always
reaching."

I got my jaws so tight at my own bumblin dumbness,
I could just drop dead an bleed shame. And stumblin like
this to the master! "Your soft sound just sends me," I offer.
I'm shakin my head to show him the *uh uh UH* bliss he
can bring.

And he sends me his smile. "Just a quiet sound. I'm
looking for something *soft* right now. Like the little puff
that the lady puts on her pussy when she cleans up and
shit like that? That's how it's gotta be. Only soft eyes for
me." His rheumy eyes damp down with long-distance
dream. I recollect what he's told me before: *"Seeing is
believing and hearing is a bitch."* He segues back on a
bridge to the text of our bandy-talk tune. He's been where
roots flower from dark ancient rain. Smiles hard at me,

focusin. *(See?)* "You lookin so good, Kit, you *hard* on a man, espeshly a old hand like me."

"Aw, you try to Sealy each woman you see."

"You must be daffy." He grins at the rub. "You tryin to needle me?"

"Just tryin to help. You know I got ears just for 'Go, so I wanted to warn you, don't try to snow me."

Old Prez's charmed an he lets it show. "I oughta slap you out from between your ears." He raises one hand.

"Look out now. You been into them goofballs again?"

"Listen at you. You talkin boo, gage & reefer? I ain't no hophead you know."

"I'm onto you, Prez. On the real side—you with me?— See, I'm talkin *oil*." I'm leaned in, maternal. "You oughta cut that juice loose. Or would that be too much like right? *I'm worried bout you.*" I could kick myself for frontin the maestro straight to his face. I'm so damn dizzy I can't seem to quit while I ain't dead. But Prez takes me easy, just like he jams on the stand, bendin round detours upcoming, flowin like sorghum round roadblocks right up to where sweet darkness ends.

" 'On the real side,' " he mocks in my own waspish way. "So why are you going to get into it and say, 'He's an old junkie. He's an old funkie. He's an old flunkie.' And all that shit! That's not nice, you know. Whatever we do, me *or* Lady, yes, she's still my Ladyday and they're down on her too with that hearsay shit. Hearing aid. It don't go like that. Whatever they do, whoever it is, let em do that and enjoy themselves and get your kicks yourself. Fuck it, you dig! All I do is smoke some New Orleans cigarettes, that's perfect. You know, no sniff, no shit in my nose, and nothing. Still I'll drink and I'll smoke. . . ."

"Well, that's your business."

Prez laughs. "Ain't nobody's business if I do. But a lot of people think I'm on this. I'm on that. I resent that like a bitch. Don't put that weight on me. I know what I'm doing. Kitty, take it from me. I don't walk around sighing the blues and all that shit. I'm like any other colored boy back from other folks' war." He chuckles a moment, lookin far off. " 'Now am I home? Or am I just *back?* Your point of view is all up to you. And these true blue billyclubs and yankee nooses, they got their notions too. *But!* '" He lets the word strike an then trail on its own in a weird offbeat way. He looks for a highball an settles on mine; takes a long draught . . . drains it near dry, then holds up the empty glass toastwise toward me. "We spoze to forget all that though; be happy to be here; go for the okeydoke— it's all ivey divey. Sure thing," he says quickly, soundin high gear. "Okay then, sweet Kitty. I'm in the breeze."

"Have a heart, Prez!" I call to him.

"That's my ca*lam*ity." He turns back to dig me, then full tilt, he's gone. But hold onto your cap, up steps Sassy Vaughan with her octaves of song so elastic; she's been wendin her way through the scales on a bender like five-an-dime plastic, heedless of poor fools like me. All we doin here in the cheer zone is sharin her spree vicariously.

"Whatcha know, Kitty?" she greets me.

"All I know's what you teach me."

She laughs; so do I, but I'm close to my focus.

She catches my eye. "Well what'dya think? I'll ask you, not the boys— They tend to see me just as I am, only today, except Mr. B—he sees my *will be,* so he tends to my druthers, he opens up wide, lets me play with a song—"

"—an the band tags along—"

She gives me the nod. "What'dya think of my chance for a gramophone date just for me?"

"You mean minus your showcase, the boys in the band?"

When she turns to glance back toward the band on the stand I make out a set to her chin an a do-or-die glimmer that brights up her could-be West Indian skin. She lops me a look just to check my attention. "Here's the hit hierarchy, take it from me: first the swing bands, then the black bands, and then come chanteuses of color like this one you see. . . ."

I'm startin to brood in a mood of *How can we janes get a toehold on destiny? Who knows the answer? Whoever it is, please be the first one to notify me—* Thoughts such as these come unglued and aloose in melee when "Hey, Sarah!" Dexter G calls from deep in the throng, and she sets sail to greet him cause he must be lonely for *legato* largess just like his own. . . . Then just as I'm farewelling S.V., what's this, don't tell me, but up jumps young Miles ("Sweet Kitty! What's *happ*nin?")

"Come again, dearheart: *you'll* let us know when you're up on the stand!" Stitt, Dexter G, an Ivoryman Hawes—that's all, countin 'Go, of the Unholy Four; they stir the sax stew outa Mr. B's band. But grab what you got, nab a seat, Jack's back on the stand with his singlenote riffs rollin loose as juice from cooked goose. You tell me, who works those high-register squeals like Jacquet? Jack, go to town! I mean paint the town *brown!* . . . "Sure thing, Kitty, gazelle," he blows like a bat outa hell, and I can't help but flow right into his mode, *screebop, seree . . . WHOO* (high squeal) *wheeeee.* . . . Just coast this roll straight through heaven's sweet gate, see just how true bliss can *be!*

It's when Jack's just stepped down and the band's swung back in time that a scramble in the rear of the club causes jazzful heads to turn an dig— It's 'Go that's the cause of commotion—'Go workin up a storm on his horn on the sly so it seems to the greenies that just don't know 'Go. . . . While we eased off into Jack's hurricane sax, 'Go's packed *his* ax and's snapped it together in view of hipsters who—what else can they do?—they lend bent attention to what must be a preview of coming attractions; they already know it so can't help but show it as 'Go takes the stand, smacking a quick kiss at me for good luck, then Wham! Spliddledy jam, here it is yall, nothin but light-happy liquidy sound, 100-proof joy on the run, notes riffin for fun from down in a cave *à la* Dex Gordon, now up into hard droppin stop like the bopster called Yardbird, then easin on over an out in a long blowing gale of a waillll. . . .

'Go's redeemed . . . so am I. . . . I've jumped from my seat to my feet from sheer burstin cheer, happy as a fat cheese-factory rat—itchin to hug that brass brilliance of his. When he breaks from the stand the band's expanded its sound to fill all available space on top of applause 'neath which Mamie's started to croon her way through *I didn't know what day it was . . . You held my hand. . . . Warm, like the month of May it was . . . and I think it was grand. . . .*

Yes yes *yes!* Here comes Christmas: 'Go headed toward me with a just-for-us grin; I can't wait to be in his arms. . . . Before we connect though he's cut off at the pass by a grey chick done up in a clingy crepe frock, an the two of em shoot the breeze in the aisle for a while with heads tight together, cohorts in scam.

"Nothin's *to* this," 'Go's already started to clue me. (I see it today, shoulda stiffed up an dug it back then, but at the time I'm just thinkin, *Girl, don't you fret, don't get upset;* but man how I've had it with runaround love!)

The floor show'd begun, Baby Lawrence was tappin to a frantic secret beat underneath the tune's topcoat of rhythm— Look at him go! No doubt about it, this cat put the "d" next to "-a-n-c-e. . . ." Then next thing I know, 'Go's standin next to me, all set to make a fast break (has to "end on a high note," he says)—

"We'll be back!" he mouths to somebody nearby.

"Man oh man, *when?*" shouts a wag in response.

"Just dig us Round Midnight." 'Go grins, an we're off to the races, already on track, makin our break from the gate.

Amazing Grace

& Saving Face

KAT
San Francisco, 1990

It threw me, my mindplay all weighted with strangers at odds in the forties, yet here's where I first saw the beckoning bet—*You a muse-ician, so musement's your thang. Bet you can't hang an be cool 'nough to see what the muse of the soul's got to show you!*—the bet being tucked as invisible string through the seams of these soon-to-be ongoing dreams. I was lured to a challenge that deeply involved me in some sort of dare that could serve as the gate to my own further fate. There was something in wait at the end of these real-seeming fantasies, something to unstop my musical block at that time when I couldn't compose, some sort of herald was waiting to guide me through dreamscape to creative flow. Already the visions had caused me to face my worst fear: I was real-eye/zing now that I hadn't composed anything worthy for days, which could've been why, I thought then, the strange chain of scenes from flybygone times had surfaced in mind to fill in the creative blank where my real spark should be.

It's at this point in progression that Chloe was on her way over—we'd become fast funnin buddies, partners in crime in no time, Chloe with penchant for critical comment at whim-given moments, despite irritability flushed up from nowhere, a drag. "You so judgmental!" I said to her once, though I too am guilty of constant critique; I know it myself, so I oughta take heed— My very same flaming advice is repeated to me by loved ones like Nate at every available interval, at each bend I come to in the onwending stream of my days in the Now.

Chloe was late and so this time I'd called her to inflate the girth of our earlier plans or maybe say "Later! I'm gonna go 'head and *raise*, I'll go solo, I gotta get outa the house." When I've been in the crib all day dabbling with ivories it's no time to visit right here at the scene of my crime. My workplace and livespace are one less-than-show-case two-room apartment with view looming outward toward wild blue Pacific of streamy dream schemes to break free of ingrown stultified life in San Fran at long last. Land-bound? Not me, I refuse to be landbound for long, which is why I insist on maintaining my own mental mecca of island design where I tramp in bare feelings, freeform type sand. *Loose*—call me loose, a loose woman of desperate intent bent on/determined to muster events of adventurous nature so's to waste not a drop of my own lopped-off life cleaved from the integral Whole.

"I'm an adventurer!" I cried to myself one time in a dream and felt pleased; I awoke with a thrill still enchanted by in-sight, real-eyes-ation that retreats from the light and

so takes place on q.t., i.e. only at night, when consciousness sleeps and unconscious can come out to play, night's
her heyday, hey *hey!*— She rubs her wise eyes with fast
fists and she springs to her feet: *Well all REET*, she elates
and so celebrate-says. . . .

In the same active night of my sleeptime before I'd
had three or four dreams, including one brought by Maldorer, the gremlin who oversees mischief in my apartment;
he's an invisible imp who runs the place, a phantom su-
perintendent not far removed from the realife building
super who's also a phantom (he stakes his claim in phys-
icality but can't prove a thing re his actual workings in
same). Just let your icebox break down, which mine did,
as humdrum relief from dull daily life, a respite supplied
by Maldorer and ignored by his cohort, the flesh-and-bone
super of clandestine cackles he smothers with hand turned
to claw soon as nobody's looking, claw-cackling super
who's crouched in cahoots with Maldorer down in dank
depths of free enterprise. . . . What I think is this: One
demon's the flipside of the other, the super and supple
Maldorer are yin and yang of balanced malfeasance, something rare in this world so a thing of beauty really, or at
least a thing of surprise! type amazement; there's Maldorer
to fuck things up, and the super to see they stay fucked:
two tireless tricksters of equalized weight in disintegrating
terra loosa, our globe, unfurling farflung as it rolls who
knows where?—through vast fiery angrified planets we
shame and make mad due to foibles of Earth, the problem-
child planet that always draws more than its share of attention.

On the day he first came to the fore, Maldorer appeared in the guise of an evil freezer fairy—he'd slipped

into this role or ruse on October thirteenth when nevermind other folks' Fall still and all it's the hottest damn day of the year when Mal rears his unseen sunburnt head in order to damage the freezer door by causing one of its tiny integral knobs of adjoinment to weirdly freeze and then break itself off in what seemed as a consequent way. Then seeing that this was done and it was good, next Maldorer punched a series of sprightly buckshotlike holes in the freezer's rear wall, mini-pock pits just tiny enough to have giant rumbling ramifications such as shutdown of the whole fed-up unit, the fridge.

What could I do? I broke down and called on Mal's pal, the sly-sneering super who came in a flash of sixty-eight hours to clomp in and See. What he saw or reported was this, with giveaway grin of complicit compliance:

"Look right up close here," he told me. "See this sticky stuff?"

"I don't see— *Where?*"

(Sharp breath) "Right here!" (tapping plasticky wall with forefinger tip containing retractable claw)— He'd seize me and shove my head into the freezer if he could without pesky payback by finicky criminal law, so sucks teeth instead and says to stupe-me in dupe tone of voice, "Here! Look . . . right . . . *here.*" (taptaptap) "This liquid, it's coolant, like Freezone. You see?"

"I dig." (And what's more, I saw it a long time before, just wouldn't admit it, caught up in feelingful thought as I am of *Fuck you, Maldorer, you and your chosen stooge counterpart here!*) Then comes the subsequent bout with my landlord that brews up to shouted / screamed threats of eviction— He's spouted and sputtered as soon as I've read him my list of losses to be deducted from forthcoming rent.

See what you've done? No joke now, I warn you, Maldorer!

Shhh. . . . Then comes silence so still that no doubt about it, I make out his shriek and cracking-up cackles of crackling free glee.

This sort of havoc, it headed my day, which is to say the previous teeny malfeasance opened my day up before me. I'd been awakened by a long-distance phonecall from Nate still away at his wars of ethnic recruitment. . . .

"I'm o.k.," he said, "still fighting the good fight against muddle-American Way."

"Where are you though?"

"I'm here in No-Motown, Detroit. It's all gone to rack and high ruin. The plants are shut down, or cranking out chevies with fuji components."

"How're the people though?"

"Eaten by zombies, most of them. The ones left can be divided into two groups: (1) Warm, and (2) Dead to the Touch. The first group's shown me what's left of the town and hugged me to their compound bosom, which is ample by the way. I've never seen so many cornfed women in all my born days. And huskytime men too, for that matter; the 'burbs are overrun with gargantuan Euroes—Poles, Slavs and Czechs for the most part. WASPs seem to be on the decline. Their eyes in the city look as haunted as ours in the 'burbs. Folks I've met here seem to have a sense of their own native culture, though, so don't hike your nose at Detroit just cause it's bleak as a gremlin's convention. . . ."

Nate had his dream; it was deferred and rechanneled into plantation service at Townsend Behemoth where, he maintains, the myth-factor's fecund, yea-high and applied

to him at importune whim. "To my secretary I'm Mr. T,"
he once told me; "and to the V.P. above me I'm Heathcliff
Huxtable. To the handful of bloods I manage to hire and
keep on the company ship, I'm Spike Lee.

"I wanted to be a lawyer," he said. "So I got myself
on as a student intern in one of these law firms. Which is
when I found out the truth about what it takes."

"Whatever it is, surely you've got it, old Nate." I
broke out in my just-us-pals grin.

"I don't know." Nate shook his head slowly. "What
it takes is your stamina and your ideals and the sense you
have of your qualified self. I was a senior in high school
and I'd read on my own for good measure; I was reading
stuff that would buoy me, you see, when I found out that
even Paul Robeson was shoved to the outpost in his law
clerkship during the thirties. The law partners figured his
black face would anger the judge. Now here's a guy who
was Phi Beta Kappa, All American, a *cum laude* grad outa
Rutgers, an orator, a statesman, a kingpin thespian, a
vocalist *non par.* . . . I don't know. I just don't know. Not
much has changed." He looked down at poor city crabgrass
knotting its way through a thicket of sad urban sod.

I wondered at his contest with held-to-chest getbacks
and wondered how he'd learned to tell when he's running
on Full so that he knows when to pull out to the side or
change course. "You're not confrontational," I said to him
then. He laughed right away with that crustacean humor
of his. "I'm alive and undoped and unjailed and I'm all
the way *well*, well damnear. When you see a brother like
me, he's confrontational. I"—he took five to look up and
away—"I just choose my battles, that's all."

It was thoughts like these that assailed me—thoughts

of brute facts and reckless opinion, *which I won't let stop me!* I *de facto* scolded myself and yet then after playing with Plexus my heartstring piano and feeling no news coming through I'd determined to leave the apartment as soon as I could. Yet then Chloe'd called and wanted to visit— she had Things to tell me, she said. So I'm cloistered in maimed frame of mind when I do as I'm wont to in troubling times: I summon my antidote: sure cure-all muse-ic to loosen my blues until Wango! Like jinxes, they're gone.

> *I . . . didn't know what/time it was*
> *till I . . . met you. . . .*
> *Oh—what a love—ly time it was,*
> *And sub-blime it was tooo. . . .*

Homegirl was on KBRO-Radio cookin up a storm, playin the stew outa cool Ladyday and rappin herself up from Warm Simmer to Boil: *"Why IS it folks always talk about what a shiftless life Billie Holiday led, how she was drug an doped out when hell, Elvis was an all-out junkie, Marilyn too, but you'd never know it! I'm a lil sick of that, now how about you?*

"Tell you what, we got two, hear me, two free tickets to give away today, they're to Craig Harris in concert with Tailgators' Tales, two Thursday night tickets to the nine o'clock show, and they'll go to the first caller who can correctly i-dent-ti-fy Ladyday's particular rank in the heavenly choir as of this moment. Is it Cherubim or Seraphim? And—hear me now—which SPECIFIC vocal division does she shine in?

"You gotta tell me how you came to your conclusion— We're gonna turn this thing around right now!"

Then she launches into "Space Is The Place" by star-guide Sun Ra and his solar singers who swing in on top of the minute:

"*Awwwww, don'tcha knowww SPACE IS THE PLACE! Don't you know? Don't you know that? . . .*"

(Music fades down, rumbling under Homegirl's re-entry.) "*All right. Caller Number One, you're on the Air!*"

It's during this nexus that Chloe arrives, dressed in magenta and talking much stuff.

"Girl," she said, laying her bag down (it being Frisco MOMA design, splished with splashed paint), "I don't know bout these *men.*"

I settled back in my seat just to listen. "You know what?" I said to her. "You oughta fix us some tea." Thank God I treat guests as family; elsewise I'd never be served. Chloe, she rose to the privilege, rushed to the strip of my studio kitchen and bustled therein, stopping but once for direction—"Where's your Red Zinger? No mind, I see." She brewed us a thing of hot Zing and poured it into two chosen cups, one from New York that Nate brought me ("Mind Your Own Fucking Business," it read), and one of orange vibrant hue which pictured four bulbous aliens seated at the edge of their own planet's turf. They're watching earth self-destruct down below in a luminous spray of splayed nuclear clouds, and "*Ooooooh!*" they all say. What a once-in-a-lifetime fireworks display. . . .

It's all over except for our whee! shouts of glee, but then—

"Girl," Chloe said as she pulled up a pillow/sat near me with my newly-rolled *j* and my red steamy tea. "Where to begin," she went on. "See, Kamau and me, we almost came to a partin of ways. We'd been fightin as usual, then

we'd made love. His attitude seemed to be in a slope; I
don't know." She looked off for a moment to lose her
distress, but a furrow of anger'd formed tween her brows.
"I do know *I* ain't got nothin to do with it. I'd just told him
he needed to get past passivity an work up some shows for
himself an his art."

"You told him that, just like that?"

"Well a course. Truth is the light."

"Well to a degree, depending on what you're braced
up to see." I looked at Chloe; she'd rushed on right past
me.

"He told me I'd gotten all hincty, ever since I got my
exhibit in gear." She laughed to herself. "The man is
con*fused*—"

"Well, hey, aren't we all."

"Not me, honeylove." She flared for a flash at the
thought. "I know *just* where I gotta go."

I noted her spontime-type fire; the uppermost tips of
her cheeks had flashed red by the time that she said, "If
it wasn't for Sadiq to take the edge off my thang with
Kamau, I don't know how I'd manage to keep myself sane."

"Smoke on this, sister Chloe—" I passed her the joint
and a nod to the wise 'cause what she'd confided had routed
me into recall of my own derailed situation of then which
was freighted with strife. Being blocked and unable to come
from my music had caused me to seek out a man—so went
the formative plan skein I schemed that snared back in no
time to bind me. My net problem was this: Not being able
to settle on one man had caused me to settle for two in a
blueprint both vague and reactive, a downsliding strategy:
Two wrongs make the right man for me. So sharing my set
at that point there was Karl, also Vide (pronounced "Veed,"

with the same ease of "steed"). Vide's red and rhiney, a
brown-freckled mesomorph with 'fro of raw auburn and
open-faced smile of gap-toothed delight, a snatch-happy
freak who openly flaunts his favorite fetish; he brandishes
it like a badge.

"Excess is as American as the Gettysburg Address,"
he said once, looking up at me from the V of my legs where
he's made his home— He's probing the tip of my clit with
the point of his rough-surfaced tongue, tastebuds pro-
truded, irritabrasive. Vide takes his time languidly licking
the lips of my hotspot, tasting the juice at its core . . .
lingering there at the well for a moment, then cool-sucking
cream from my innermost soul til I wheeze in the wake of
warm lava that sails me through serious bliss to some other
evenkeel shore. He lingers to savor the flavor of afterglow,
nipsipping gustative hightingled spots til I give up/let loose
and laughgasp for mercy: "Vide, are you hip to all gone?"

"Too much is enough," he suggests, and leans in with
languor for more.

When I picture Vide as an object, a thing, what I see
is a big bowl-shaped drink on a glassbrick thick stem—a
cocktail concocted from four different juices and three
kinds of liquor plus peach pieces, pineapple bits, and hard-
kernel stultified cherries. . . . Sugar encrusts the rim of the
glass, and from deep in the lushhearted heart of the thing
spring two friendly straws for two oneway trip fools.

Thank plucky fortune for balance of Karl who's Vide's
flipside, a boiling pure double of volatile one-five-one rum.
Karl's hairycurl chested, medium height and dark as tip-
toeing welcome black night: an Honest Man Who Works
With His Hands— Somehow Karl conjures this image and
works it to death, despite his role in real life as an actor

with spangled potential in Follywood's dull Milky Way of nebulous nebulae. With his keenfeatured face and all-bizness body, Karl puts me in mind of a creamy-type dream I once had. . . .

Lost in underground passage cluttered w/ construction debris where tram let me out. Kind-muscled workman comes to show me path of escape/blowtorches opening we climb through together. He holds me close/guides me from behind through narrow straits, holding my waist w/ one hand, feeling near walls w/ the other. As i walk forward my hips sway merengúe/brush his hardhewn thighs with their bough in between. In rushhhh of breath—feel his grip on me squeeze/feel my pussy flick-signal in reflex response. We tense til i turn to look in his eyes and see me gaze back: tall willow in peach muslin shift w/ tan tinge of my skin showing through just to outline the curve of my calves/bowl of my butt/pears of my breasts w/ their stiff raisin nipples.

"Welcome!" i smile, but

                "Wait!" he confides; "I'm Adam; you're Eve with your leaves of free women to come," and he leads me to ease-trickling stream where he bathes me with cool fingers and smiles at my heat and then splashes a handful of fluid into my soft core: "Let me kiss you." He draws my hips to his mouth/eases licked lips to the node of my nectar/sucks at my sap in warm whisper of time w/ its sinuous rhyme til my calyx releases its savory flavor and

     MMMMMMMMMMMMmmmmmmmmmmmmmmmm

"I want you to know, it's not something I ordinarily do, but I'll share this with you. Are you ready?"

I try not to, yet can't help but see it as Karl rambles on on the day he'd come bearing a screen treatment he's

written— Karl appears to me in rerun of himself at the
Lodestar Theater in offbeatway downtown San Fran, he's
trundled on stage wearing a cast-off robe and scapular in
his role of mediocre missionary in Erskine Threadgood's
Les Noirs— I see Karl crying downstage in a relentless
pan-African accent, "There is no excuse for hypocrisy! It
is the impotent tactic of cowardly minds!"

Then comes a vision of Karl at his best, magnificent
as aging weathered Makak in *Dream on Monkey Mountain*,
Karl unrecognizable in costume and vigor, with knarled
network of grizzled grey beard, brows, sideburns, and
epaulets of hair beside bald pate. . . . What's more, he's
undone his front dental bridge for the part. . . .

Uh-oh though, can that applause— Here's Karl again,
resurfaced in *Stoned to the Bone*, a fiasco he's written,
directed, produced and PR'd; Karl in deadbeat drag as a
ruffled Frisco transvestite on a street known for its stock
of peddled pastime wares.

"Karl?" I sliced right into his pitch, no holds barred—
"What made you pick the dragqueen for your one-man
show? Did you catch any flack for that?"

He wrench-looks away with furrowing brows and lips
clamped together with such force that pressure manifests
as two ashen points on both sides of his mouth. Yet when
he swivels to face me a few seconds later, there's only the
twinkle of his miraculous dimples flanking a wide-bright
smile of his warmth.

"The transvestite came to be involved in the sketch
to represent people who're alienated, who're struggling to
find themselves, whatever they think they may be." He
pokes at me playfully, looks up in thought. *"How can I
say this? [strokes minimal beard growth as tacit cue to*

dubious muse] The transvestite is an archetype. He's a [pause]—a symbol of people who're trying to develop that ME-FACTOR, regardless of being outcasts in society. [with somber severity] I get the feeling you're not taking this seriously. That you're kind of . . . laughing behind your hand or something. I tell you my dream, and you . . . [looking away with downcast eyes] I'm hurt. [after pause] I really am."

With premeditated remorse I move toward him to cradle his head in the sling of my arms, stroking corkscrew curls at the nape of his neck where the sinews descend to night-colored skin. My fingers etch care with taut strength of their own, lean ladyfingers secretly wired with biscuity pith, kneading the pain from tomorrow's refrain. Then I ease into apogee, full-pageant fantasy.

—*I see you wrapped in brown silk or fur or feathers about yr caramel face & shoulders*— *I see you that way too, my Mahogany MysteryMan says in my dream, in the way of a poet by trade or by desperate defense.*

—*I've got to taste that voice, i think, and the view through my fantasy frame shows another frame visible from the other side of Now. MMM has one phallic finger finding me or what makes me tick at the time; my my instant jackpot which i bingo! deactivate so as not to come too soon.*

I titillate myself with a smile . . . ponder internal take-off and external thrust. MMM touches the trigger in my hotseat, just to see me fire.

—I can taste the honey in your skin, *says MMM. (I send something juicy back for his sucks.) One tongue. Joint node. Our oneness that feels like molten gold looks. I fly from the world with this knowledge: I can be activated any time/any place/by any one of a series of serious poets who know what remains to be seen.*

"Do you have a pen? You better take this down!" Karl was urgent, inspired by a surge of wild thought.

"What did you say?" I'm all ears and acidic attention, all set to dig The Idea, Karl's Idea, and to give him my *take*. Then's when he mentions his goal: a TV series he'll star in and manage to get to Right Sources on the yellow brick road to the promo rainbow.

"The plot hinges around a detective who's also a bagman for the cops and a hitman for the mob," he says. "He's a black guy in his thirties, virile but not macho. If there's injustices or unfairnesses that are applied to people— things society refuses to deal with—then that's what he's up against. He's anti-racist, anti-discrimination, anti-sexist. . . . He's really a nice guy see, and he wants to help society, but he's caught up in the day-to-day hardcore reality of life in the ghetto—"

I cut him off at the quick in his thicket of themes. "Do you see any contradiction between the character's aspirations and his physical, I mean his concrete, circumstances?"

"Not at all. Life's full of contradictions, and so's day-to-day life in the ghetto." He smiled from his chair down at me on the floor. "There's a girl in the plot; she comes in when somebody gives the guy a marked bag of dope from Bolivia by way of Brazil—there's a political dimension too, see—contra and resistance interplay with the CIA's role brought in as a catalyst, a *key* catalyst—"

"I see. Do you think one of the networks would pick this up though? They're not big on black Ramboes—"

"He's not Rambo! Are you listening to me? This is a guy with a social conscience, a guy who thinks on the balls of his feet. He's forced to wage a personal war in the streets of his community. . . ." He clamped his lips shut. He was running his hand through my bandeau at the back, now and then snapping elastic into my skin. I slapped at hishand.

"Look." He waited a moment, then snatched back his fingers. "When you *grow* enough to know to support me, you know where to reach me. I'm gone." He grabbed for the teak Kenyan cane he was sporting, tucked it under his arm, and played his way to the door.

Sidelong Flings,

Ecumenical Things

Whaaat you gon-na . . . do for me?

Chaka sassed up through a groove in the Bose on the floor where I sat swami style—Vide had brought the tape long ago: *Chaka Khan Lays Em Low With Her Soul* or some such nutritionless goodie, but man oh man what a full-flavored taste! She couldn't carry a tune in a truck but Chaka knew how to *job*, to nervesheathe those notes through your raw tangled ganglia. *Well all RIGHT then, Sis! TELL it!* I yelled out and jumped to my afferent feet set to dance. I pretended to search through my halter and shorts, then ran hands through my mane of wild hair caught in its snare of elastic. . . . I would've gone on to mime Chaka fur-ther—it's hard to resist when my mind's full of sisterly Chaka, she-wiz of vocalsoul biz, indomitable Chaka golden-ascended from oldie Back Then, from the time of my roguish teenhood when her sole competition—this to

my yet-to-be-purified, peer-attuned ears—when her sole
competition was minikin Minnie Ripperton sighing her syl-
vanly songnotes spritelike in air at a time of my urgent
hormonal despair.

> *You can come inside me/you can come*
> *inside me/Do you*
> *wanna come . . .*
> *insigh-ide my love?*

went the jam that I'd chosen as the theme of my youth
when I hated and feared my own relentless innocence.
I remember thinking—this at thirteen and headed down
the street, smoking a nervous Pall Mall— *Ya know, I*
should get started NOW. That way I can't get pregnant
since I'm not on the rag yet, and the early bird doesn't
get tagged. . . . I couldn't wait to deflate my distended
virginity—it stayed on my mind, weighing me down; so
three years later I sought out an unassuming young thug
of my choice, a cream-skinned muscular boy who was so
bad he was ripe—It was he who I set up to (*yeah!*) take
me off. . . . I just hadn't thought of the where or the when.
He knew his cue though, Donny did too, to the point that
he thought he'd called it himself and he set me up, when
the truth of the matter was he followed through.

But then here it comes, Feature Two, the ambush
remembrance that sears through the rest, it calls me right
up to the edge of my mind: *Remember when you were raped*
by that boy you wound up with one miniskirt time? "Want
to go to the show?" he grinned to young me in flight from
the torrid-zone clime so I jump up as is and dash to his
car— Just the breeze of the drive is all that I'm after and
all that I dig as we speed past nabe after nabe, and then

past a faraway exurban mall. Ahead is long-stretching brown ground in the distance, a stillness of people, a building decrease—("Hey, where we goin?!")—my first intimation that the show is no go, uh-oh, but too late . . . he's pulled into raggedy X-rated drive-in of cars crammed with belligerent billhillies, enemy turf of off-limits K.C. The next scene's a chase atop padded square feet of desperate car seat— The guy's got me jerked in a neck hold, twisting nerves in my throat when I move: "I'm gonna get you, baby," he lets me know. "You want me to use a rubber or not?"

"Use it then—" This last comes out choked with a piercing of pain, a preview of coming detractions about which I make up my mind then *I won't tell a soul; they might won't believe or 'll think I brought this mess on myself. It's my last time off duty when it comes to my safety, I promise, dear God. . . . Just see me through this and I'll tighten my outlook, you know it, I swear.*

But teen life, she loves happy flipsides flippant enough to balance damnnearly the load of your blues, which is why I suppose there were also those golden-oldie yummy times when I'd sit with my Donny standing before me in frontporch feverish heat of my Mem-mothered home—I'd sit on an outreaching ledge with its jagged brick edge pressing skin of my legs in their summary mini, feeling no pain but the joyous fatigue of the tease that I busily eased into being. . . . *Just raise your leg a bit so the lil skirt slides just so to the side— See? He's jumping out of his skin for you—* He was a swain in the habit of smiling at me and then leaning toward me in friendly fashion to ply me with kiss after intimate kiss; he'd suck my lips open and suck in my tongue so that I tasted my favorite flavor, cum-creamy seemed-to-be love.

> *Tight fit,*
> *Tight fit,*
> *Do ya have thuh*
> *right fit?*

Ask Chaka; she knows how to savor such sorts of sustainments, sostenutos of senses and such, and she shows it right now as the doorbell, it's ringing, announcing Vide's visit on this day of frolic, my *trente*-type birthday, *mon anniversaire.*

"Happy Earth Day," he greets me. "Sweet Thing, I'm so glad you came to the plane!" He sets down his gifts, the standard libations, a fifth of rum and thin packet of coke, and he sets about clearing a place for himself on the weary loveseat. "Come here, Babes," he arc-waves to me once he's piled up the *Voice* and *Bay Guardian* and saving-grace pages of *Be-Bop And Beyond*, nevermind heretofore segments of each; he's joined them together in one motley marriage. "I've got something to tell you." This last he breathes out in a rush, patting his knees as my tentative seat, a gesture I note and file to accommodate later, 'cause right now I'm busy making one of my no-goal rounds of the room, a circular movement of body and brain trained on axial thought. Around and around she goes, and where she beams down, nobody . . . Vide knows I tend to revolve in this matter—"skittish" he calls me, no matter—

"Get to this," he says further, caught up in urgent-type thought. Instead I pour drinks for us both. I don't know, I've got something in me that auto-resists, it makes

me so restless with confines, a trait that was spawned with
the rest of my neuroes during my Mem-mothered eager-
beaved youth. In the larger frame or loom of my kidhood,
this was the time of Jackie Stone's house in kidhood K.C.
where we all convened after school—this when caretaking
Mem was at parental work, overtime hospital shift in long
shrift—when unbeknownst to protective Mem, my pal
Jackie's joint would be jumpin with at least two friends
each for eacha the seven sons and daughters involved in
the family revelry. Music would always be poppin: somebody would've hit the hi-fi switch earlier on in the day,
somebody there on another tour of duty—there were three
steady rotations comin and blowin; I was part of the next-
to-last round, I fell in in the early evening every day, right
before dinner when in self-defense Jackie's mama and
daddy'd clear the house while they all grubbed downstairs
before they'd let the fest resume. Meanwhile they'd send
you outside or to Michael and Allen's room way upstairs
in the attic with its soundbox that Mike and Al had pieced
together—whoever was up there with me and I would've
started it unbidden and turned on the blue bulb and toked
up the herbaltea smoke or at very least stoked some Pall
Malls, whatever was there, along with whatever liquid re-
freshments were newly contributed: some Gordonsgin or
Fleishman's in that nubby ice-lookin bottle, a half a pint
of that or some Ripple wine flavored grape or sweet
cherry— Two or three girls countin me'd be there, inquisitive types who wouldn't take No for a tip. We'd be
first on anyone's motorbike revved up an headed for Anywhere, hangin all down in the garage with the boys, watching em put cars together at first, handing em wrenches,
then next thing they knew we'd be right beside em up

under the hood/would've slipped into somebody's overalls
while no one was lookin—a blind man could see it was a
set-up, prearranged and master-planned, but nobody
kicked

cuz the girls would've contributed something by way
of admission—some hubcaps or something we'd brought
with us to donate. Once I brought a battery I'd managed
to carry; my hair was all caught in the grease of its top . . .
I was hunched to the front with a smile on my face—just
one of the girls with same spunk as the boys, all set to
funk to no-frills or junk tunes like the Vanellas' "Dancin
in the Streeeeeets!" A tune'd be groovin and everyone movin
around the raggedy livin room including Mama Stone trailing through the house with two little crumbcrushers holdin
onto her skirt; she'd manage to shake one now & again.
Her hair hangin in wisps . . . her clothes wrinkled . . . :she
was my ideal of womanly practical beauty with soft steadfast
smile of no nearby tomorrow and feminine waft of nature-
sent scent. And old Daddy S, he'd be on the back porch,
summer or winter, writin in that notebook a his, what it
was we didn't know—he'd be writing an opus, as if he was
all by himself an damn the melee, loud madness around
him—writing like he was on a desert island, just he and
a lone steady palm tree.

The music upstairs though was of a mien that made
its mark only on kids who already were *outside* somehow;
we'd decided to go ahead with what was awaiting us—we
pulled our future right into our now. And Milt Jackson
helped us, provided the theme with his Opus de Funk,
which right away opened new provinces for me/sent me
through limits of headspace so that I could hear hints of
my loosely shoed muse in the mrinngg! of those taut vibes

of his—man, oh man! Milt.— Even today, when Bags
Jackson plays, I feel blood spray through the nerve-jumping
keys of my soul, diddly ding, zring spring winggggg. . . .

And the forewinging reverie ringing from pubescent
youth is why I don't know about Vide, who spent his
growing-up years here in ethnimelt Cali where blackkids
are raised in oppressionless fiction far from blackcenter or
the sense of darkself that rides high by its side. So in his
deeds and his softlife delights Vide's an *assimilato*, a cul-
tureless case of amorphous i.d. With his upgrowth like
topsy in silicon Oz full of zombies and zonies all blonded
and bronzed with their overblown muscles and nosecone-
type tits, what could Vide be but identity-absent, an un-
identified flying blood/U.F.B.?.

Vide pulls at me. "Where were you?"

"I zoned for a moment." (But then I'm in Cali. What
more can I say?)

"When we're born"—he skews in to a distant
drummed cue, using his body to illustrate high-interest
words: brings "born" to life as an arc of his arms with head
bowed, a priestly gesture that posits him again as the
seminarian he once has been—"When we're 'born,' what
we really do is choose to incarnate."

"And what can we do but use what we choose?" I
snapped to attention as if I'd been called, and made my
prodigal way to the folds of his lap just to listen. I kissed
one small patch of his tan-bristled beard, and seeing the
square where shaved hair met the side of his chin, I light-
licked that righteous spot too. I wouldn't miss one of Vide's
sermons—they're chock-full of gospel, no jive, and what's
live is their hook to a dream I once worked while completely
awake— I'd partaken of some of Vide's blow at the time,

snow-white snuff that twinkled like Christmas at noon when I suddenly saw what I'd wanted to see: my own sacred fantasy, which I offer up to the rest of the flock here and now. (We all need redemption!) (Can I get an "And how!"?)

I feel my MysteryMan's wand in redeeming folds of my flesh, hard stiffness in my envelope, as I squeeze out the miracle juice of the moment and make it my pietal own. MMM calls me *angelica de terra* in delight and pontifical joy. *Omnia secula et seculorrrrummm. . . .*

What I want is at-onement, with sex as a sacrament: I slide back into now-time like dust on a dime only to find Vide scoping me with care, he's twining one hand in my squirrel's tail of hair and's started to rough-tug for inclement attention—("Hey, lighten up!" I manage to say.) He pierce-looks at me unflinchingly. "I'm just trying to put you in touch with your feelings however I can."

(Hmmm, I don't know though. Well, maybe. . . .) It's one of the hazards of dreaming in public, crude interruption that wends you right back to the cavern you flew from, currents of care that wrap you like air; others' concern for your rational welfare: Here. Let us help you to ground! Vide must be one of these earth's deputies, *id*spatched to my case in disguise—

"That throw you off?" he was asking.

"I'm with you," I mutter through miff. " 'We choose to incarnate.' And what can we do but our duty?" (Our dharma, task-karma. I think of myself and my own stopped-up musical charts laying in wait just to tease me. Somehow I've gotta express me, gotta come from my secretive soul-fuse with beckoning internal muse.)

"Now there you go, Sweets." Vide was allout delighted, massaging my knee in his glee. (Why wasn't he thinking how haplessly pious he'd been?) "And that's just the point, don't you see? It's like you with your need to make music. This life's just a field trip, you with me? We're only obliged here to chance some adventure and draw some conclusions."

"Then to report back to Headquarters."

"Exactly." Instead of a mad, he'd put on a glad rap to foil me. "When we're 'born,' we just break off a part from our ongoing life and express that bit in the flesh."

"Why use bodies at all?" I'd spar with him yet.

But he's all set to block and to jab me right back: "The body's our tool."

"Like a barometer?"

"More like a probe." He pressed testament lips with their border of beard to the back of my neck with its nerve cords of hadbeen resistance. I had to proceed though, to take up the thread of a vestment of thought I could hear in my head.

"I'd've rather stayed . . . gone," I went on and said.

His mouth played with a stasis a moment. "That's what you say. The ego," he laughed with a catch—"What does it know?"

"This 'field trip,' you call it, it feels like a sentence."

"I wouldn't say that." He slapped hard at my nose with the bush of my hair.

I ducked just in time. "Well I would."

"This life's just one of some possible options." He gave me his wait-and-see stare while he quickslid his hand from my knee to the welcoming lace at my flange of scant panties. I could feel his big thumb rub back and forth under patient elastic, felt my neck being nuzzled with textural strokes of his bristly chin hair til I'm inched up to high rough Enough. But no time for taut thought of halted momentum, Vide's kneading the mound of my hotspot, testing for moisture and warmth; he's a senses bent chef. His forefinger's etching the rim of my cum cup . . . it tips up to bare brim of hotsauce inside . . . then it withdraws to the cave of his mouth. He shows me the dance of his tongue at the taste. "Sweetness," he says into my lips with the stream of his breath as formative current, "I'm here to take you back out of this sphere."

Miracles

~~~~~~~~~~~~~~~~~~~

And Makeshift Lifts

~~~~~~~~~~~~~~~~~~~

I haven't posed fingers on piano ivory of Plexus for days, but in front of me via what seems as an ordinary audiotape spun into action on mild-mannered livingroom stereo, Cecil T's jumping for joy on his keys, working the juice from each piano note with a stac-ca-to tease and then *longato* squeeeeeze . . . and Vide's here for the date I've awaited, finally he's here just to see me, and to see what I'm charting perchance? (*You gotta be jivin. Don't be ridic.*) Yet nevermind Vide's *blasé* 'tude, and nevermind snared composition; there's no time for mourning lost reason for life, no time for strife of life's axial abstracts, the world of Today hates such musing so mutilates muses wherever they sneak-try to hide and to think of new ways to make way through the mire/to inspire unheard of flight patterns above and beyond unyielding concretes such as this one I'm wrenched now to see: I've just taken note of suspect provisions tucked in Vide's busdriver's workbag—a beaker, some ether, and what looks to me like a test tube of rack-em-back crack.

No doubt about it, Vide's stopped in to hit a fast few on his split shift, a casual chemist all set to cook up his vaporous brew. "All I need," so he says, "is a maintenance dose that'll help me *transcend* just enough to stay social. I'm under attack, I hope you know." He stops to laugh a black booming laugh, loud, strong, and emetically long. "Driving is hell. Did I ever tell you? Cardrivers try to get you to hit em—"

"They seek out lawsuits?"

He laughed again. "What can I say? It's the American way. Speaking of which, did I tell you? My boss is a peckerhead bigot," Vide says, and goes on to tell how said cracker has habit of notching the belt of his modus for each black he sets up and then screws via what seem to be company rules. Don't get Vide started on race-minded fools. His point's that as long as he's high, he can be *down* and not forced to vent rage on the job by menacing means, marbelling cars being one. Bitter busdrivers, he said, thump lethal steelies at cardrivers' windows nearby, mini-curveballs spun out of space from seeming no place, aimed to sidetrack a wrong wayfarer's karma. In the coast from his crack though Vide could be cool and so free from flash ire at combustible junctures of urbanlife strife. Instead of deadending at rage, he'd bend into smooth-wending detour: he'd turn the puff of his cheek to his pipe . . . wait for entry: *Open sez me; let me into my inner dope den of no din/only thin tintype peace/ceaseless flow of let come & let go. . . .*

"Katness, I know you're not ready for this," Vide was saying at standstill, still decked in his cap and brown jacket. "In the larger sense though, narcosis is contact with spirit. It clears your circuits for keener reception—"

Did he say "deception"? No doubt about it; I take it as this—(See how he's already started to grin, showing his teeth in a secretive smile?) Then's when I slam right into his preplanned agenda. "I *told* you," I said, "a thick time ago, told you straight from the gate, nobody uses my space as a launching pad. Crack in my place? That's out, man, that's all the way dead."

"Baby, look—"

"And what should I see?"

"Kat, you're all wrong."

"And you? You're all right? Man, get *a-way*."

He held up his works just to hip me: I must be square. "What makes you ready to rule on my high? You drink, you do 'caine—"

"Only on special occasions. Enough to stay sane."

"And who judges that?"

"Me in my wisdom. How's that? Will that do?"

He flash-checked his watch. "All I need is for you to let me be me."

"*Beeeeeee ... allll that you can beeee....*" The red, white and blue tune trudged through my head so I sang it out loud and then said, "Not here you don't be what *I* say you won't, and you won't be no crackie, not in this crib." I looked at him then; he was miffed, ticked, and sore.

"You're down on me? Why're you running this weird tightass energy? What the fuck's wrong? Have you had a rough day?"

"Not up til now. You know good and goddamn well—

"Want me to tell you again how I feel about crack?"

"You seem all set to clue me." He'd widened his legs

in a V as he stood, looking balls to the wall, like Macho
McKinley. *They had their ideas of how he should be should
act should respond to their hedges and onslaughts should
feel/no/who ever minded how Vide should feel?* said an
*interior voice that he'd known all his life as his own, heavy
with potency/salvaged by impotence always in wait as safe
gelded survival: the only sensible heaven.*

Where had he been? I saw him struggle to cognate;
he barely came to.

"Baby, life's short," he suggested. "There's no time
for us to work trips on each other. "Sides," he slid in,
"you're no model of coping, yourself."

I considered the charge, bound myself to a hearing:
Regardless of struggle, had I failed to *hang?* Then came a
chime from lost chronograph Time, a fractured perspective
via C.T. on the soundbox, insight disguised as a crashing
chord change that lit up the way back to *now,* a boon for my
stye-clouded Gemini's eyes. "I beg to differ," I said with my
hands on my hips. I felt suddenly stiff, not like flexible me
heretofore. *Just leave me alone with my muse-echo high,* I
thought then. *Don't try to clench me or clamp me to bunk like
your drool for your junk. I've got my own craves, don't you
see? I'm a slave to strange streams of the past and I'm
blocked, truth be told, from my musical hold....* But fuck
alla that, I felt called to cut in, "Vide, read my lips. Take
that kit, get that shit outa here! And hey, I know what.
... You can split with it." Inside my mind though, I put
it like this: *Later for you and your dues; I've got blues of
my own. Look at this man,* said the voice in my head, *he's
strapped to his bag fulla parasite need that'll never let go—
Need won't take NO for an answer, ask any leech; it'll say,
"Has my host still got juice? Well then, hey!"*

Vide was beside himself, bent out of shape. "You know what? You've got a full dose of butch bitch in you."

"And you got some bastard in you." No sooner'd I said it than Vide laid down law by way of the sting of his slap on my face so that inside me, in dense tensed-up time I hear dissonant wildness, C. Taylor's matrix-note thickets, springtight arpeggios all set to go. When I focused on Vide he was looking at me in a seethe-heated way that fired up my flare and we scorched straight ahead. "Fuck you," we said at one time. I chimed right in with bad Blood, cut him no slack 'cause of what I'd boiled down to: sugar that's burned til it's realdeal and sassy, carmelized to the point where it's all the way black.

I was looking around me for objects I'd use to add might to my frail bantam weight—the rod from my easel was one; I wanted a *gun*, then felt *Hey, this ain't me! But it CAN be*, said a deepseated internal voice and I had to agree, so went on to say my due say by the way: "Where the hell you get off, hittin on me?"

"Do unto others," Vide said, which led me right to the edge of this suicide fantasy: *I wrench the door open, rush back for Vide's bag, which I throw down the stairs with a loud glassine clatter— His pipedreams are shards now, all in a shatter.*

Vide stared at me. "I just could stay gone for good."

"Would you do that for me?" I gave him a fixed thin-rind grin.

He zipped his bag up, tucked it under his arm, and made off just as mean Cecil T had stopped milking each key of its hidden-stash rash harmony.

MODE two

Snowbound Dues,

Red & Green Blues

KITTY
Kansas City, 1945

The night fog was cold, riding the wind like the breath of a demon when we hit the street. Yet 'Go's square hand's in the air the moment we split, an no sooner does he signal than a taxi appears from nowhere, skids to a stop in response that's the norm of respect that rolls up to 'Go like to no other Negro I know. If only he'd put his head where his heartfelt music is—life's too quick to burn to the wick from both ends; she'll see you in hell first, show you who's slick. I can't help but think of 'Go's model, seemin-old Prez, his lost bout with booze an its ooze through now used-to-be life. . . . Next I see Fletch, in flow and fast ebb of his genius, wrenched to the bend of extended dead end due to No Thru Traffic, not for a cat of his hue.

'Go looked at me suddenly, like he felt my same itch of quick-warning alarm, though he goes on to slide his

saxcase onto the seat and to usher me into the cab with
its radio syndicate blast:

*. . . and so tie a string around your finger, don't you
forget this upcoming Xmas night at Carnegie Hall, as we
present the most senSAtional and wonderful concert ever held
in exciting modern progressive jazz to-NIGHT, the twenty-
fifth of December, Saturday night of the week; we hope that
everyone'll fall by and dig everybody—the great Dizzy Gil-
lespie, Charlie Parker—everybody's gonna be there. Remember tickets are available at the Carnegie Hall Box Office
and right back there at the box office of the Royal Roost.
We're gonna take you diRECTly to the Royal Roost on
Broadway now in the wee small hours of Xmas morning—
to the Royal Roost, the orig-gin-nal metropolitan Bopera
House, where we take our WMCA microphones to bring you
the finest in modern progressive jazz, some of the greatest,
featuring the wonderful Mr. B!, Billy Eckstine, the sensational and wonderful Charlie Ventura and his gone group,
and of course the great Bird, Charlie Parker and the All
Stars, who you hear in the background now doing our theme
tune, "Jumpin With Symphony Sid." And I know that we're
really set for a won-der-ful morning, a brand-new Christmas
morning, headlining a 1946 year that I know a lot of you
frantic ones out there will really enjoy. Here we GO, ladies
and gentlemen, this is the VOICE OF AMERICA bringing
you Charlie Parker and the All Stars with the great Bird,
Kenny Durham on trumpet, Tommy Potter on bass, Al Haig
on piano, and Max Roach on drums, doin a little thing for
you that I know you'll shake a leg to, "Groovin High!"*

The cabbie turns to face us; his eyebrows say "Where
to?" and Chicago, he hips him with no more ado: "To the
Ville, jack. I'll cue you from there."

"Sure thing, mack." The taxi was winding through reams of sly ice in sheet after sheet of sleet frozen fast by dutiful nature—it can't help but seize a freefall and shackle it to time. "Was I hard on you tonight?" 'Go was asking; he'd picked up my blue attitude. I was down in the dumps an he knew it, so he'd looked at me intensely, then he'd looked away.

"How you mean?" I just say.

"I had it in mind you were sore."

"Cause a what?"

"Ain't no tellin." His face went frigidaire cool. "Maybe you're roiled over Mamie."

"No such luck." I met him head-on with my lie. "Think I'm screwy enough to think any sad skirt can work her way next to my man?"

"I got eyes for nobody but you an you know it." 'Go stroked my neck, kissin soft sorry kisses into flash heat of my skin.

I boosted myself into a smile. *A man's got a mind*, I was thinkin. *Can't nobody take what's not willin to go.*

'Go was pressin sure tips of his fingers into my shoulder . . . he quick-licked the lobe of my ear so that fear flushed out through me like rain down a drain fulla wide-open welcome. I felt his breath warmin thin skin that rounded above my gown's bodice, felt him lower the search of his lips to the upper curve of my bust, felt me slide to the edge of self's sand shift til I discover/can see that Chicago's not with me, he's dishing me up a weird chin-up grin, then he leans toward the cabbie: "Corner of Newstead and Grand."

There goes my bliss; it sinks to my shoes—I'm wise to that spot in the Ville, it's where they all score.

"You sure you want to do this?" I hear myself ask him words spun out as reflex and already reeled back by his reflex response:

"Just let me make this run," he says as a statement, no by-your-leave is involved. "One thing you need to know about me is I'm *grown*."

That does it— I force myself to let him alone.

The wind had started to come up again; frozen stars winked in the icy night sky.

"Don't needle me now," 'Go's saying. He gives me a small cut-dry smile.

"I just wanna give you a hand."

"When I need your help, I'll hip you to it."

I wouldn't let up. "Spoze I get hip to it first?"

He looked at me hard. "You want a kid?"

I got one, *I thought*. He's disguised as a shag-tempered man. *I look at his profile angled in anger that pinches his cheekbones an hard-carves his chin.*

"You chock-full of mother tonight."

An you empty of that, *my head says.*

A glint sparks his cat-colored eyes an he blinks like he's heard. "Anytime you get sick of me steerin me," he says slowly, "don't hold yourself back, just give me the word."

Think again, I wanted to yell to the lug. If you steerin you, hell, you could've fooled ME.

And here comes the fool I don't want to see. . . .

The cab's no sooner pulled to the curb than outa nowhere comes the connect, catwalkin with a hop to just within view of the ride while 'Go coughs up coins to no-concern cabbie, who soaks up the hint: *Buddy, I dig; I'll be cool.* . . .

"You rang?" the goods dude slides words to 'Go.

"I'll take a *tres*," 'Go lets him know. When 'Go turns his back, I lose my momentum, slide outside of the moment to where the quick loop of life, it catches me up in a vine twist of themes that grow from my heartslant toward 'Go. . . . *'Go's slope into nowhere in rest-stops tween fixes of music and boo.* Is that the tune I'm on my way into? Somethin too stuck in the blues draws me to him, makes me see death with a grin on her skeleton mug fixed at me an I see one shinin hell light beamed at 'Go too.

"*I can let you have a quarter. It's only a bill.*"

"*I'll go for that.*" *'Go's steady chuckle, too loud an too long.*

"*This stuff's tops, pal. You can bank on that.*"

The chase of "All Too Soon" wings by in boptime of my mind and neath stronghead saxes I run through my personal turn-of-thought snags, the maze is familiar. . . . I know me an my own need that drives me: I want to be the life of this man, his indemnity plan for all the changes and bridges left in the tune. I want to be the heart of 'Go's solo, the lone note that glows with his brilliance that feeds me an already bleeds me. . . .

"We'll fall by that new club, Ace High. You with me?" 'Go asks. The mooch's slid back to the crack he oozed out of, an just scope on 'Go—already he's eased; his skin's regained color, his fingers are sure when he reaches to button the top of my coat against the night air. He's taken off his muffler an's windin it onto my head as a turban on impulse so screwy I feel myself smile too easy, too free: You got me; you know it. You know how you gas me.

Bigtime Jazz
& Razzmatazz

How you feel? 'Go told me once about a middleage woman who'd befriended him in the thirties when he was just a teen on his softhearted own an lookin for something to do with himself— The woman had approached him with this question. She was all done up in jewels, furs, an 100-proof perfume, comin at him on the corner in front of the Reno Club on the upside of Beale St. in K.C. Prez Lester Young was playin inside, a cat 'Go had wanted to dig but'd been cut off from hearin in person because of his scant shortpants age. He looked the part of a junior flip too, gangly all-bones but still fine, I'll lay bet, an ready for *an-nay-thang*, preferably wrong.

"How you feel?" She strolled up to him, him alone then as was his bent, even back *when*.

"Who, me?" He could've kicked himself for the chumptime response, off-cue an late, just like Pop always said. The lady just smiled though, a credit to her mild-chill demeanor. "Sometimes," she was to tell him later, "it's time to just shut up and watch. That's a little-known secret you folks need to learn." At first that threw him off, with her bein so lightskinned that she could pass for white, but then he learned to take her crispness for just what it was: her effort to straddle both fences at once—the wood one to one race, the barbedwire to the other, an to maintain some semblance of savvy meanwhile, to maintain some . . . just to *maintain.*

He spoke up to let her know he had sense. "I'm tryin to get in to see Prez an the Count, but I gotta wait for the okay." He'd let her know he had things underway. "They 'pose to be lettin me know."

"Oh they are. Who's this 'They'?"

He was shocked. Everybody colored knew who 'They' was. *You must be jivin,* he thought to himself.

She was smiling at his thoughts like they rode the airwaves, broadcast to sundry an then some. "Don't use that word around me please." (What, *they?*) "It calls to mind servants and masters. I don't wait for pronouncements from Them, and I don't pine for their by-your-leave, or mumble when it's missing. I don't look up to anybody . . . and no one can look down on me. Now. Tell me what you need."

He couldn't think in the wake of her words. She waited awhile, then "Stay right here," she told him, and trailing foxtails an sweetwater fumes, she rushed toward a black door marked STAGE, an whizzed back out about three minutes later. "Okay, we got that out of the way. Here, take my arm—I need an escort. You'll do." She laughed and guided him forward, 'Go walking dumbly, numbly at least, led by this patronsaint woman who's nameless an smooth in the groove of his feelings. He was all set to quiz her he

said, when through big double doors up ahead music
washed out in a tidal wave toward them—Basie's huge
sound swelled up in a roar. She stepped up her pace with
him at her side now, him proud to see heads turn and
hands waved to the woman who'd torn off two comp-ticket
stubs and stuffed them into the usher's late hand. 'Go had
to measure his bopwalk to maximum cool, had to stride to
keep up with this slickchick mystery on cute platform heels
headed forward: "Good, there's a table," she said.

Where? The only free seats he could see were way up
in the faraway front of the place. With her in the lead they
scrambled like squirrels through a forest of knees and bent
shoulders ("Say 'Excuse me,'" she clued him without cut-
ting slack in her progress) til they reached the end-zone
table in no time and sat there like a queen and her dutiful
king.

Everyone near was dressed to the nines; they all fell
out in gladrags for the occasion—dandies duded up in big-
knotted ties/chest protectors flanked by flat-map lapels of
double-breasted suits. A few velvet-collared overcoats
rested near some of the sharpest-togged cats. . . . He leaned
to check detail and found what he'd hoped he would see:
lisle handclocked socks, tucked into Stacy Adams and
Florsheims—fine fancy kicks for cats on the move to a
groove of their own, independent and dapper, on the upswing of Crash times. The Depression had pressed its last
choking breath, it'd eased the death grip of its claws even
there in the Ville where he and Pop lived, eased leastways
to a degree and the world was rid of war forever. It was
like the old song he'd heard when he was nothin but a
hightopped lock an stock kid, just a bruiser, a baby— Pop
said she didn't, but he could remember his mom sang it

then when the stock market crashed an folks of all kinds hit the streets on the make: "Happy Days Are Here Again!"

Women's boxcut crepe shoulders rocked to the rhythm around them, and here and there a fineframed dame's cape sprouted lush ostrich feathers or reddish fox fur. When he squinted his eyes, all 'Go could see was an ocean in motion of cloched pin-up cuties in jet beads and what seemed like one long twisted rope of freshwater pearls. A dream come to life—Duke E's "Black and Tan Fantasy" in waves of skin shades tan, black, and beige, nutmeg and cinnamon, coconut too, and coconut milk like his friend's. Light-complected chicks with their blue-hued dudes, brownskins with browns, mellow browns with hot-chocolate blacks, ebony dishes with ivory cats, all toe-tappin in time to the swing, all the same. Prez had sashayed his sax to the mike, easing into liquid lilts that bobbed like buoys on a bountiful bay . . . then Buck Clayton blew in K.C. Style/riff to solo/ trailing a sassy bright kitetail of brass, and 'Go could hear Helen Humes's lighthearted lyrics bounce in the breeze of the Count's punched-up background licks. . . . *Life can be SO sweet . . . on the sun-nay side-a the streeet!*

Leave your worries on your doorstep. . . . She called him at home the next day, at his Pop's. "Hey now, it's me. What's your agenda on Saturdays?"

He was put off by her abruptness, the way she seemed to take over, so he tried some tactics of his own. She must be misguided, due to mosta the men bein away overseas at the front when she was his age, comin into herself—a common hazard, Pop had told him when he talked about those times: World War I, the Men of Bronze's triumphs in Champagne and Munich and Jim Europe's glory, first

on the bandstand, then as combat commander of world-
famous black troops who were originally assigned as Labor,
men used as mules, so went the plan til need forced re-
thinking—"Necessity's a mother," Pop said. In those days
of the War to End War women had had to jump behind
lathes and factory vats, so they couldn't help but flow into
fantasy manhood though they had no idea what the status
required and no one around who could show em, 'cept Pop
an his fellow 4-F'ers. "An we needed a break; no way we
could do for em all," his Pop laughed. But—

What did he do on his Saturdays? "I got me some
regular duties," 'Go told her.

"Such as?"

"Well, me an my boys fall by Too Short's to help rack
em back for tips in the poolroom, then sometimes we fall
by the gym. Hardy don't let us spar, but we get to pick
up some lightweight technique, an we get to be in on the
happs."

"That's good for a start," she cut him off. "There's
somewhere I want to take you." (Than, to his pullback:
What's the lick?) "I guarantee you'll like it. Have I lied to
you yet?" He heard the smile in her voice and could picture
her then, the way she carried her height like she'd bought
a corner of the world an was layin odds on the rest. The
way she walked straight-certain forward, her manner more
like a charge than a walk so that ordinary folks felt her
comin an adjusted their ways to allow for her presence
among em. He thought of the way she wouldn't take No
from nobody, laughed at its hollowed-out sound, said it
didn't suit her, said all her options were tailormade to fit
by her and her alone. The way she didn't grin an skin in
company, colored or white, just nodded folks into the know

with a crisp no-juice smile. How she *listened*, even to a youngblood like him, as long as folks were sayin somethin, an was quick to put their nonsense on the shelf if they weren't. She was straight-backed and lean, on the slight side, her wavy hair thick and gloss-black, piled to one side in an offbeat pompadour that made her look tall-tree terrific yet ready to bend in strong wind. A flexible twig of a woman with all the oomph of an oak. And—well he was a man, or damn mannish—those beestung lips of hers rouged to a frenzy of like-it-or-not—she acted more manly than any chick he'd seen yet, all while lookin the most like a woman.

She could've been as old as his mother; he couldn't tell. Women with their makeup an tricks— "They can be old as the jungle, you'll find that out, an you'd never know it, thanks to Max Factor—" Pop had told him this when he was only six and Miz had left for parts beyond. "On the lam, and don't *give* a damn," Pop said back then. "Your mother is a rollin rock, just as self-centered as any one man. Can't stay put up for long. She was tourin with a road show when I met her, an kept on tourin all the time in her dreams an ambitions, nevermind wedlock or youngster to raise, an nevermind me, though I got her a job just to keep her, one a them choice gigs as a elevator operator in a plush-time hotel way downtown where all the girls got their hair done for free an free makeup jobs as parta the package— They all had to be light skinded; light, bright an damnnear white—the crackers love our brightskin gals. All she had to do was stand there crisp an cute all the goddamn day, just grace the premises an bring home her pay—an know what she did? A groundsnake'll bite your hand every time— She went an hooked herself up with a grey dude, the same guy who run the hotel—he offered her a spot as his secketary an she jumped straight to the bait, knowin full well colored gals cain't be secketaries, not in *this* world. She even went to bizniss school, passed for white to do it, then bought her some eyeglasses to go with her act. Tried to look stuck-up, all kept to herself; nose was so high if it rained she'd a drowned—all this scam for the 'fay boy in order to be his priverate goddamn secketary. They was private all right, they better be an they knew it, but I didn't know it, had no idea *what* she was up to, never tried to rein her in so she kept me in the dark, just her fool. Then one day Wham! up an gone with the ofay to a parta the world I'd never heard tell of, to somewhere I was hard put to find on the map; nevermind you, nevermind me, nevermind who she was supposed to be—just like that, little man, like a train takin off, all booked to spout smoke one minute, next minute revved up an gone. *Watch my dust.*"

'Go couldn't get over the way that she'd left him, couldn't sleep nights for damn near a year, wet the bed, an that could be why he'd started to stutter—Pop's friends, women who took care of him, always told him so. They'd cluck over his lean longboy ribs an shake their heads sad to themselves, "Such a shame!" They'd make bigdeal noise about his "condition" an go to lengths just to feed him ("Gotta put some meat on those bones!"), til he thought he'd die of their manless attention, directed at him by default.

As for his new friend, she'd taken him to the library, a squat squarecut building on Sixth St. an Front. "Nothin doin," he said when they'd walked to the door, an he'd leaned forward an seen the lame inside of the place just as a full-fledged fool was on his way out. "I ain't no book bait," he told her, "take it from me."

She just smiled an stayed friendly. "I knew it," she said with lowkey intent. She was pleased with herself, but not pleased for long because—

"Get this," he told her with strength in his voice which was leveled low now, he just hoped it held—"I'm not no sissy now an I don't plan to learn to be one." He'd floored her with his uppercut wit; he'd lay back now an watch her recover, so went the scheme he'd concocted, but strangely enough she didn't get sore.

"Tell you what," she just said with a tree-steady look at him looking at her. "We'll go in for ten minutes, and if you want to leave after that, that's exactly what we'll do. Now how does that sound?"

"Sounds like a hype's how it sounds. Look, I want you to know, I ain't all that green, I'm hip to some grooves. But just to please you I'm willin to swing wit the program."

She nudged him and grinned. "You've got more nerve than the law allows." And then to herself: "This is *bound* to be fun."

He'd come away from the place with a tall stack of books and a kids' picture dictionary—books like *Up From Slavery* about the life of Booker T. Washington, a dude who'd wrenched himself away from the deadend he was born to—an interestin break of fate, fantasy to young 'Go's frame of mind at the time. BTW to him was a male Cinderella who'd been his own fairy godfather by need or by choice. Now that role rang true an familiar—Pop'd hipped him long ago how black cats were the original do-it-yourselfmen of all time: "Hell, son, the motto of our race is *Ain't nothin to it but to do it!*"—a took-for-granted inside anthem that kept all blacks on our track, the mystery of cool and its flipside, *make-do*, though 'Go didn't know how to call it back then. He'd gotten the Booker book along with a mag about W.E.B. Du Bois, a white-lookin colored dude who'd set up the Niagara Club to turn Negroes around in their chances and choices of life in the mainstream, whatever it was— It was this notion that caused the light-skinned cat, W.E.B., to be all over his boy Booker T. Then there was a third dude named Garvey who was anglin for a share of folks' minds, *Black* folks, he called us out loud with nerve to be proud—Garvey said what Black Folks needed was land of our own, startin with the turf in our heads. Garvey'd taken on the whole U.S. of A. with his go-for-broke thoughts so that now he was dodgin shellfire from the G-men; but still the cat stuck to what he knew to be true. All the fuss over ideas an ideals—it was news to young 'Go that notions themselves could cause such a ruckus, men's muscular notions of change. . . .

"Why don't all these cats come to grips with one groove?"

"As long as we have more than one head among us," his older friend said, "we'll have more than one way of life."

And *how*, he thought. Look at Pop an my mother, his up-and-went wife.

"All those leaders do have one thought in common—the big one, their goal." She was watching his disbelief. "Oh, that's a fact! The one aim is there; it's just hidden by the different ways and means."

That's enough of this, he thought. Too much jive got him down in the dumps so he cut her short. "Yeah, well this cat Garvey, I'll lay wage on him."

"What makes you say that?"

"Cause he's in the know. He puts his money where his mouth is— I dig the way he's pickin up all that lean green as parta his plan—"

"Contributions you mean? Oh, he's no crook now—"

"Who said he was?"

(*The FBI, for a start.* She just grinned.)

"He's leavin all the thinkin-cap cats in his trail, I know *that*," 'Go went on. "He knows what he wants, to duff back to Africa. An he's all for gittin while the splittin's good. *Look out, I'm comin through!*" 'Go couldn't help but yell it out, he'd let himself flow into Garvey, his schemes became 'Go's. *"Build me some boats! I gotta get hat! Nevermind the fatmouthin, later for that."* He pretended to jive with ole tired Booker T. "You can put down that hoe, pal. Colored folks wasn't meant to be farmers, we got us some big times in store. An you, W.E.B., bright-skin boy, we don't need no trashtalkers like you. Who wants in with the 'fays anyway?"

She cut him off in midact "I don't know about *that* now; that's not a fact."

"I was just razzin." *This chick was sharp; she don't miss a beat.* "You had me thinkin spades should do what comes natural."

" 'Spades,' *hell*," she sliced out. "Speak for yourself!" She pulled herself back into shape. "All I'm tryin to get you to see is how Negroes can't afford *not* to be aware of our choices, at least til we straighten things out. Du Bois,

Garvey, *and* Booker T— As far as I'm concerned, we could use some of each."

"You said it!" He'd fallen in step with her tune way too quick. Ain't that a blip? He'd square things away . . . give her the slip. "You said when we left here, we'd move to *my* groove."

She pursed her lips an then smiled. "I seem to recall that."

He shifted his books and put one arm around her waist so that now he was captain in charge of their course. He smiled over at her an she halfsmiled back in a way that unsettled him; his gladness was jarred by a jolt from the depths of his memory, way out beyond his empty-sad now times. . . . Still, he leaned over toward her an quick-kissed her cheek. "Now it's my turn to hip you to somethin," he told her as he took the lead.

"That's fine, I'm with you," she said. (*Yes indeed!*)

Side-Bent Schemes

And Straight Ahead

Dreams

'G O
K a n s a s   C i t y ,   1 9 3 6

The malt joint was packed with wall-to-wall faces as far as the eye could see though the center of the room was loose with with-it stragglers who'd bopped to be closer to the jukebox, dancing or no—none was allowed. The boppers were rockin with slick discreet steps rigged to juke music rendered as— Wait, a joker's just dropped two bits in the box and the first jam of his ten turns out as "Stardust," with wild Lionel Hampton working up a lather on his alltime vibraphone. . . . He took a look at Lena to see if she dug, but she was looking off to the side, seemingly elsewhere by choice. What did she have on her mind? Whatever it was, Hamp went on to work it away, Hamp ridin in on a crest of wind with Willie the Lion Smith trailing a kitetail of sound underneath him, Blahdadat,

doot*dee* do, blahdadadat do-doolie wahhhh—*split*teledy
bah. . . .

Aw, prick your ears to *this* goodness! Jump an jive
for kept-alive joy in the face of your race to the contrary,
nevermind blues of your layaway dues, just listen up and
get straight to this: Slam Stewart walkin this way on tight-
struttin highsteppin bass, with Charlie Shavers shavin the
stew out of curves in the melody, he cuts corners *close* in
a skinburn skid of pure risky glee. Look at me! He can't
believe it himself (Tell the truth!) how his brass notes, they
gloat past the traps of the band and this land, leavin a trail
of pure sass, schreedidee *whee*, bopdopstop. Young 'Go
stepped on it hard then—he had to hurry to find them a
table near the jukebox itself with its lower-deck speaker
woofing for all it was worth, in a war with the tongue-
waggin jokers all over the place.

He found them a booth with its own baby jukebox
there on the wall, had to elbow past oglers and loafers to
cop it on top of the moment its occupants split. "Come
with me," he beckoned to Lena, who seemed in a daze.
(*Thought nothin could faze her! Well, she's human too.* . . .)
This woman, well, she wasn't like ones Pop had warned
him about, the chicks Pop pulled his coat to were des-
peradoes in feminine form, all set to separate a sucker
from his dough and bump his head to boot. And well, she
didn't seem so razor-edged that she could slice through a
heart, or your head for that matter. She was bold enough
though, she had enough punch, and her words packed a
wallop you felt to your socks; but one thing: though she
must've been upwards of thirty, she came across as trueblue. She seemed braced and angled to head fullsteam

toward what she believed in, no matter how many hurdles stood tall in her way. Every time he thought of her so though, Pop's words flashed back to light up his foolish faith. *"Women are flighty an think they almighty. Take a lesson from your ma—What you call her? 'The Phantom!'—an see just what you kin expeck when you give em their head. Any fool can see that—blind, deaf, or dead!"*

Yet this particular chick, this lady was some other breed. He'd help her, impress her—he knew what she needed. At the next booth a couple sat down, and shine seemed to follow them: the fella was pressed an ace-dapper, his head conkoleened an his dish there beside him with readgleaming smile; the bob of her hair was buffed up to a sheen. He caught sight of the waitress, who frowned at his nod, knowing that now she'd have to leave her post of goodtimers jiving beside her; they took the pricks out of a pincushion gig.

"Two concrete malts," he told her there at their table. "Doubledose fudge."

"I gotcha," she said through thick bubblegum. "An what for the lady?" She chewed while she waited, eyes focused Elsewhere on Who, me? beyond.

"We'll take em *today*," he ragged her, no fuss—he'd be his own man, *Don't take no stuff, an stuff don't take me.* "What's the damage on that?" In her ranked offguard pause he paid her four bits and waved her away; then he slanted a glance at his friend to see what she'd say. *I'll get a kick outa this*, he was thinking only to find her looking away, her eye-easy profile angled to view.

"I had a little boy once, just like you," she'd begun. "He'd be your age now," she said to his startled resistance. *Little* boy? *Come again!* "I still think of him as little . . .

mothers always do." She smiled past his eyes, peered into distance behind him so that he was prompted to turn to the side in order to see what she saw. He could see only head after shiny waved head, bent to malt straws or hotdogs or tilted back in blasting black laughter. . . .

"He used to be the light of my life. . . ." Her voice trailed off into nowhere, twisted in dark roots beyond. "I used to, we used to—that boy could have had anything he wanted from me, it's just that I—" She looked at her hands with alarm, at the malt straw they held. "There were some things I had to do, and he . . . . Well he left me, that's all."

Ladyday's croon trickled in then in a thin, haunting strain of meandering pain, each note a gnarled link in a seaweedlike chain. *"You doe-wan know . . . what love is . . . un-til you've learned the mean-ning of the blue-woos. . . ."*

"How could he leave you? Thought you said he was only a kid."

She winced at his quiz in a squirm-restless way with a look of caught-culprit surprise. How could she put what she knew into words? The boy wouldn't know what she meant— *But you do*, said her own voice within in relentless refrain: the dullthrobbing ache of a warwound— How could she say she'd been wounded in battle?

'Go cut her off. "The kid's father, he quit you?"

"In a manner of speaking. I left him first, is the way most folks see it, but consider the source: Most folks cut you no slack, not in your motherhood, as long as you're able, especially if you're"—she went on and said it— "light, bright, and damnear white, their image of uppity, seditty . . . *'You must think you cute!'*"

She sounded sad and roughed up, tough in response, and 'Go couldn't help but think it: He'd done it again, whatever it was, he must've, when all he wanted was to give her a hand. What had he done? He lay his longfingered hand on her slim one, his tan topping her toast-tone-hue brown to lighter-weight brown, two sets of thin straight-edged fingers with lean oval nails, his slightly fanned in proportion to hers.

"Do what I say, woman! You the man now?" Mee-cham's raspy-toned drone coursed in her mind. But then in its wake came the image of Meech when she'd met him, soft-spoken, quiet, so still and reserved on the trolley beside her, squiring her to the new colored talkie by what was his name?—by Oscar Micheaux.

"He didn't understand, my boy's father, so I had no choice but to— I did it, I chose to do what I knew I should do: I packed up and left for the green I thought I had seen in my future." She chuckled to herself in a spent flinty way. "Sometimes you can't stop for the go-ahead; you'll find that out in life. Other folks don't understand your dreams, so you can hardly expect them to flag you in to your own personal finish line. You've got to do what your own inside voice tells you . . . and nevermind folks' bitterness, calculated or not, nevermind how they misread your dreams— You can't expect them to get ready for what you're hardly ready for yourself." She pushed the words out in a small private voice. "You've got to stride forward toward whatever it is that destiny's seen fit to leave on your doorstep, be *you* at all costs, the best you.

"Folks have never been ready for me. " 'Girl, you crazy!' " she mimicked in sudden singsong that stopped as soon as it started. "I was crazy like a fox. Amazed myself—

I didn't know I had conniving in me, but they drive you
to it, I swear! You start to come up with ways to get around
them to get to your goal. I didn't know I had tricks *in* me,
but your knowhow expands to fill all available space, and
I'm here to tell you, I popped off the pot top from mine!
No sooner than I'd imagined what I wanted and made up
my mind that it was for me, opportunity rushed up and
presented itself, it snatched me up by the scruff of my
sight so I couldn't see anything around me but it, the *ought*
of my life." Her words were unraveling all on their own.
"Ask me again," she said, more to herself than to him.
"Ask me again and I'll say it some more: Do what you've
got to do, take it from me! As for other folks' ideas of what
you should do, if they don't jibe with your agenda for you,
well, use their low-fence ideas as stone steps to jump; they
can help you pick up momentum. You grit your teeth and
push to get past them, I do at least, and I can see we're
alike in that leaning."

Who, me? he thought then, though he could see how
Pop's lowboy ideas somehow never depressed him, even
the old man's rundown about Chicago's own ma gettin her
hat an decidin to duff on her own time, nevermind his
needs or Pop's for that matter— Somehow 'Go never could
drum up hard hate for the woman, 'cept at times he was
already down. Somethin else weird took the place of the
hate, somethin offbeat an strange, a screwball feelin of
out-of-place pride. What should he call it? Admiration
maybe, grudgin admiration that ground through his gut to
get out; he was secretly proud— He liked how his mother
had handled herself.

Sound filtered up from the jukebox, the rasp of Ladyday's tired-teenage voice with its blunt edge of premature

pain. *Why peo-ple* tearr *the seams of oth-thuh folks' dreams.
. . . is o-vah my head! . . .*

"That's how *I* feel," his new friend said.

"You an me both." He looked at her hard. "What happened to your little boy?"

She looked away for a taut stretched-out time— He saw her shoulders sag under the weight of the truth. "He was cut off from me," she said with no warning, straight up.

"How you mean?"

"He doesn't know me, never knew me, though I knew him. . . . I know him now."

"Come again? You lost me." *Enough of this run-around, the whole thing was screwball, right off the wall. What in the world was she trying to say?* He'd noticed that grownups had a hard time with the truth, it grieved em real bad like too-narrow shoes. They were much more at home with their tailormade lies. . . .

Ladyday's voice sifted up like unruly sand. *Do nuth-thin til you hear from me. . . . Pay no at-ten-tion . . . to what's said. . . ."*

His friend was looking straight at him, as if she could see through to his tangle of thoughts. "What I'm trying to say is, since I left my boy, his feelings for me have been dead—"

"What makes you say so? He'd be his own judge of *that.*"

Then's when she lost patience or poise with her ploy, he couldn't tell which. "Listen," she said with stiff lips. "I left the boy when he was only seven—walked out the door and never looked back! How else could he possibly feel?"

'Go took the lead. "Ain't you jumpin the gun an playin im cheap?" *Here was somethin he knew.* "Maybe he feels just like me. My ma left me—" He glanced to the side but his eyes danced right back despite the sure bet of a getaway. "Look," he went on, and said to her. "Why not try to contact the kid? Give im a choice. What's that you said?—'You just never know til you try.'" *He had an idea; it flashed in his head like the Fourth of July.* "I'll even talk to him for you—"

"You've already done that you see, you just did," she cut in on his notion; her eyes were all dammed up with tears. "Little man, my Chicago, I've loved you. For years."

Montevideo:

A Road Show

On Leave

From Chicago

LENA
Montevideo, 1933

Bobby Tucker vamped in on piano underneath wings of Ladyday's singing—he folded her blistery whisper into his dark cape of chords: *Don't explain. . . . Fire/don't explain. . . . Skip that . . . lip/stick. . . . Don't/ex . . . splay-yain. . . . "*

Ladyday's clairvoyant voice and its channel of keys— It put her in mind of how it was eight years ago when she'd first left the boy and his deadend papa called Meech. It seemed like a dream, *was* a dream in its impact and scope, a dream full of mystery figures materialized from the mist of a predestined future she saw no need to confine herself in. Her lot as she saw it should stretch far and wide; her plans for herself rolled right up to the edge of *I Can* and couldn't be wound to round backward. What she was for herself was one way, straight up and over and out if need

be; finding herself on the outside of other folks' tired ex-
pectations wasn't news, it was norm, and so were folks'
frowns at her freedom to dream. She never did know when
to ask for permission, missed all the cues to say *please.*
She stumbled right past polite time to curtsy, to Them and
to those of her own kind who saw fit to tie her or try,
seemed to scoff at their ways of plowing spent ground for
its patient permission, tilling tired soil for long-dead go-
ahead that never would push forth and bloom. Her way of
taking for granted made her seem like she thought she was
wondrous, or white. Whoever heard of a colored chick,
seditty and onery (she must be) and still with her feet on
the ground among earthsters, still with her footsteps right
among theirs til she took off like Earhart, light traveler in
bold solo flight?

She took off in flight to the height of her dream: so it
would seem to the few who would see the whole scene from
her lean point of view—

"Why'd you bring me here then, if you didn't want
me?" She pitched this query to Cam who shelved it at once
out of reflex, then couldn't resist rising to bait that was
whiteman's delight: the chance to get some Negro *told*—
Good Lord, how they loved to instruct. She and he were
in Uruguay at the time, there in that suite of Camvren's
Hotel Björn with its front-slated view of the aviary, a
brilliant-plumed world built on stilts.

Cam sized her up with his eyes as iced as the *fjord*
whose shore he had come from. "It takes a weak man to
not know his feelings. I am not one for letting myself take
me by surprise." His skin had mild-reddened, and snowy
tinges lit dimples flanking the smile that caused his cheek-

bones to jag up to their summit. "When I came to your country to seek my prosperity, potential was boundless for any earnest hardworker like me."

But not for Meecham, she knew. . . . She recalled when she'd met Meech there at the 1918 fair in K.C., him dapper an dutiful, so resolute that it showed. He'd hitched his second thought way to the North, heedless of his mam's heldback permission; he'd brought himself there to K.C. to where he stood deferentially, admiring her in the months after the scavenging trucks sent to cartload the colored had left from their plantation hunt.

"I know you're way too big and bright for surprises." She'd let him know how *she* felt; he was head of hotels, not of her. "I don't know what it is that you took me for—"

"I thought you wear *you*." Camvren said. "Was I wrong?" Again she was defensive. Her people were infected with their history in America; they wore their past as a shroud. He ran one hand through his takeover thatch of willful blond hair.

Just look at him try to look worried, she thought. He seemed like the bulk of his ancestors rolled up and tied into one knowall screwball who thought he was heir to their mission of centuries. God save us from white wouldbe saviors.

"As I vremember, you wanted all this," Cam was saying. His eyes scanned the room with its plushness of bright-patterned chaises edged with bamboo next to lush baby palms on the brick-tiled terrazzo. "As I recall, you couldn't leave the States soon enough for your liking." He mimicked her voice and her style. "'Get me away from this sad longplay song!'" You told me you'd had it with life that was—how did you say it?—laid out for you. You'd stumbled into hell with that worthless gazook you wear married to, and once you'd had the child, you wanted out of that—how did you call it?—'hammerlock' too."

He'd gone on and said them, the unmagic words that unleashed her straight-off response— She felt heat flush upward beneath her chemise, then felt herself push forward toward him, her legs in their trousers propelled her, a lifeless thing driven by rote and reflex, clattering now on wedge-heeled huraches that tapped out a tune of staccato resistance. "Who are you to spell out my motives to me?" Her full lips were compressed. "I've been doing for myself since Day One and I'll be damned if I need you to navigate me."

"I had what you needed. You wanted to sing." He was walking away, straight-backed and proud. He was no fool for a woman who bristled with quills full of quarrel with her color.

"I *have* to sing," she said then. "I didn't choose that. I have to and I have to be [where were the words?] what's in me too." She hadn't meant that; what she meant was "fulfilled" or a corollate goal with the loose hint of memory, something hard to pin down though it made itself felt in cold crannies of day-to-day life. But too late— Cam had gone on to fling the words back in her face. "What more do you want with this chip on your shoulder?" His supple lips twisted. "You are singing in my cabaña. Is that not you on the bandstand downstairs night after night?"

" 'And that's enough for *you*.' Go on and finish," she told him. "What beats me is how you know so much and still make time to run the world too." Who in the wellspring of hell did he think he was? All set to focus her spotlight, ready to train her own sight on the Lena *he* knew. She

swallowed a smile at the self that she steered, a stranger
to him, Lena the girl with the getupandgo. She'd sprung
up and gone all right, that's the green truth under God's
heaven, and heaven sure knew that she blew. Hell knew
she'd do it again, regardless of setbacks or anyone's getbacks, least of all Cam's and those of his brethren white
dipped in Right. The Ames family in her pushed her out
toward her purpose, it hustled her on toward her duty to
be here, that dutiful *Do it!*; it harried her head when she
should have been sleeping, brought her no peace/allowed
no release from the clench of each challenge that brought
itself to her for taming. "You can skedaddle away from
your fate," Minge used to tell her, "or you can jump on
an ride im right into the wind." Minge, breaknecking
cousin-as-mother and then some—she hadn't thought of
mad Minge in a while.

"When you want to do something and want it in earnest," Cam was saying, "you've got to be prepared to give
something up. Everythink costs. This, it iss true for us all,
not just for blacks." It amazed him, this uppermost focus
on color; Americans all were so dazzled by skin. . . .

She'd sunk into silence; let him think what he would.
She felt vaguely itchy all over—the tropical heat was a
predator that sucked everything in its path.

"You really should let go of those notions. They hand-
icap you. When you free yourself from your needless con-
straints, you will be free to be you."

"Gee, thanks for the tip," she said to his gently closed
door in undulant steam she could feel. "Now I know where
to come for my bromide."

'T'aint what you do.... It's the way that you do it—
She'd sung King Oliver's tune that night to the cabaret
crowd surrounded by palm fronds and blond bamboo settees
that pocked Camvren's place, made it seem part of out-
doors, of wide-open pastures she pictured leading to peace.
It was easy to lose what was left of herself in songs that
pushed themselves through mellow minor keys, they melted
like raw sugar, sharp and strong flavored, flowed from the
heart as plain harshsweet cane. Singing like this, straight
from soul's sad resources, was something that always had
called her and lulled her; it had haunted her habits through
home after home, from the homes of her growing-up moth-
erless years to the three endless years spent with Meech
and baby Chicago back in K.C. (She'd been a wife? It
seemed like a dream made of mummies and crypts that
were called average marriage, a sentence of days that were
dead but for flare-ups of fights fueled by bitter frustration
and misunderstanding— on-and-on blues wrung from day-
to-day dues.)

*"You say you wanna let somethin outa you that you
got all stopped up inside?" Meech said with his sidetwisted
grin. "That what you sayin?" She nodded, her hope for
their marriage still green at the time. Meech threw back his
head and barked out a laugh. His swamp-colored derby slid
down to the floor, and he stumbled an extra few steps while
bent in mirth to retrieve it. ("Meech, I—") "Naw, woman,
shut up an let me tell YOU." He had hold to her now, had
her neck loosely gripped in the crook of his arm just for fun.
He was nuzzling the side of her face with his leathery lips
when he broke out in laughter all over again, rumbling
reproval she felt sear through her deep inner ear. He put*

one thickskinned hand on her stomach and rubbed calloused fingers across the weft of her uniform's deft gabardine. "You got somethin stewin inside you all right," he whiskeyvoiced to her, "an I'm the one what cooked up the stew!"

This was the man she had wed, the selfsame Meecham who'd taken her for the ride in a surrey in 1918 in the days when ragtime had come to a bend of dwindling acclaim and boogey woogey'd grown tiresome and maudlin, nearing its rinkytink end—he'd had to apply plenty of spunk to arrange it, yet he was always respectful to her, cap in hand mannerly. Through his own industry he'd persuaded the carriage driver to take this chance in off-duty time that could cost him his job. Meech had three-card mollied the man in a routine game of Man Chance and claimed the favor as his only just due, hedging the driver's reluctance with, "Buddy, this is a case a necessary courtin that's gotta be took care of. I'd do the same thing for you. Matter a fact, I'm willin to help you harness the horse, an what's more, I'll take full blame for what we're go do, should any nastiness come to pass later. Soon's as I get paid at the foundry, there's two half-bits in it for you too." So Roscoe'd accepted and drove them today, the man being decked in full regal finery, gold-rope-braided cap and fringed epaulets arrogant-squared, snow-colored gloves and shiny black kneeboots as if he was driving for holiday whites.

Meech rested one hand on her small dirndled waist. "What kinda good things you got in that basket?" He smiled.

Lena raised the checkered coverlet from the reed-handled box that set at her side. "Fried chicken and some of that coleslaw you said you take a liking to." She lowered

her eyes to feelings she'd never known in the whole of her
fifteen years here in the world she'd just begun to face on
her own.

"You know somethin?" *Meech asked her, seeming all*
set to answer himself. "When you say the word 'picnic,' you
oughta know this: It came from stringin up"—*he took stock*
for a moment—"Negroes like me. 'Pick a nigger,' it started.
'Pick . . . nig.' You see?" *He studied her countenance as she*
looked demurely at his. He'd seemed surprisingly bland as
he spoke, stating the message remotely by rote. He'd with-
drawn his right hand from repose and was using it now to
cradle his ash-knuckled left in his lap.

He spoke to her softly, his words hunkered down under
some kind of grit. "I call it savagin, what they do before
an after the noosin, you know? They bring their women an
babies to see. It's their way to bring food an to eat while
they do what it is they set they minds to."

His offhanded manner, it made her uneasy, and Cyrus,
he knew what to do. In no time he'd hugged her to him,
soft-brushing the nape of her neck with his care-gentled lips.
This colored gentleman wanted her favor; he'd treat her
gently, she knew. She'd married him later that year.

Now there was Cam looking at her, stretching thin
lips in that same skintight grin. "If it weren't for me," he'd
been telling her . . .

"I'd just have *me*," she'd cut in. "I don't need no man
to complete me or be my advisor. Quiet as it's kept, I don't
need no man to tell me what I need!" She was aware that
her lingo'd slipped back to its origins so she drew herself
up to her full five feet three.

"One thing you forget," Cam said slowly with cool-measured words. "Without me as your angel, you're left flat in hell." He offered his smile as a sling for the words, he was willing to help her manage their weight.

I know what you did, for me and to me, she thought. And I know what you did that I felt myself lured to like catfish to bait— She was thinking of how in the beginning she'd compared herself to Josephine Baker, still toast of Pahree, les Folies Bergères and the rest of the places like sparkling *baguettes* on the seam of a dream— La Baker was northstar of Europe itself. She'd risen from ashes of barren background and ascended through talent to holding high court for the world's monied princes, something she, Lena, would do in like manner: she'd be hub of her own dazzled continent, glistening star of all South America, so went the plan she kept carefully tended, oiled in her mind. What's more, Lena had a head start—she'd brought her own prince to the party, while Jo'd had to choose hers from suitors sunstruck by her aura of glamour. Cam was a means and a method for Lena; she was no babe in the forest of devilish trees, never had been, at least not for long as her memory measured.

"What is wrong with you now?" Cam was at the edge of his patience; her needs were his albatross, weighing him down to a lone dismal deck. "What is it you fancy?"

"It's what I can't stand, and you know it. You prey on my nerves with those women of yours—"

"We've discussed that. I am a grown man who must have his sport." He laughed at himself. "My diversions are harmless to one who is also adult."

"You expect me to be your ally—"

"I want no more from you than you are able to give. In order to get you must give, this is no news. . . ."

"I'm fed up to *Full* with what I don't want in this world. Why should I settle for life that won't settle for me as I am?"

"Because you would have it so. You must meet new experience with a welcome." He opened his arms in an abstract embrace. "I am an adventurer." He smacked his lips against squeezed fingertips in the mode of a chef. "I relish adventure and all that it brings. Nothing is negative. Episodes all have their use."

"You suck up sensation is all, 'cause the ways of the world are tailored to fit you and your kind—"

"I don't believe a word of it." He suddenly laughed. "I am joking," he said, still so amused that cheek clefts mock-creased his smile. "I am so sorry God made me a white man. Accept my apology."

God made you a fool, she thought to herself. A bald-conscience fool or his twin. . . .

"I am sharing the fruits of my whiteness with you. Is that not enough in the way of atonement?"

When he'd left, she put an orthophonic record on the Victrola and the new Cotton Club band rinky-dinked into the room. *I let a sonnng . . . go out of my heart. . . .* Harry Carney swung Ellington's troops into a unified happycat groove. She could picture HC, the little man with the big baritone sax that he spoke through, weaving those rhythms right into your soulcontrolled toes. The way he worked his way through the registers, wove through bold notes like a serpentine herald who geared the whole world to tune into its ears. And stay tuned they did— Folks were jumping and jiving from Harlem to Hungary, doing the Snake Hips and kick-it-up Charleston laid on them all by what was her name, Elida Webb, "play aunt" of that young song-and-dance slip called Horne at the Cotton Club where Ellington now was a firmament fixture. Then the Club opened its doors to slum-hungry whites who foraged for feeling. . . .

"Shuffle Along" had been staged in downtown New York by the color-full Talented Four—that's what drew the color quest crews up to Harlem for more of the same where that joy of jazz came from, that and what *Look* magazine called "Revolt From Machine Age. . . ." Well, maybe so; it was that and highhat society's dash from the Crash that already had felled talltree free enterprise—leastwise whites called it free when they flowed here in droves from low-capital Europe, but to be in the know you had to ask colored who'd scrammed North on the mass-exit lam just like Meech did . . . and get set for an uppercut comeback. *"What's 'free'? How you spell it?"* *Free* was a word used by Wobblies and Dale Carnegie. . . .

. . . *that (oompydoompy) mel-o-dee—(roompah doom-pah doompdee)*—HC was packing his sax to the top of the keytapping stairs and coasting back down on a single slide note. When she caught herself scatting through split-second blanks of the tune, it put her in mind of Pops Armstrong blazing his trail of brash trumpeting brass from Storyville to Southside and thence on to Harlem where he was now, enthroned with his Hot Seven musical cooks and that belt-em-out warbler who'd named herself some sort of Waters, which fit her—she'd be washed up in no time. Seemed like everybody who played in the Apple got there via Chicago, which was why she'd gone to that stepping-stone city of black-market booty—now *there* was free enterprise decked out in crime—the town swamped with go-for-broke mobs, real dealing entrepreneurs with their

nightclub plantations of short-salary songsters. She'd
planned to try out for the posh Creole Show, a dance and
song ode to *femmes d' couleur,* but then came the bloodbath,
Al Capone's version of Valentine's Day, and she knew she
was through with the city before she'd begun. It was always
that way—fate seemed to pluck her right out of the stream
to her just-spawning dream and heave her toward white-
water rapids she'd begun to expect. Regardless of that
though, she'd always remember Chicago with sawtooth joy
in her heart—how songful it was a scant two years ago,
snapcappy Chicago of wild '29. Its music had drawn her
by magnet, wrench-pulled her there where she'd wound up
with Cam and his shortcut to fame—she'd make her own
name, she just needed a change that was square cut and
fair.

When you thought of Chicago, you thought of the
joydom called Jazz. She thought of this now in soon '32,
thought it again one more unnumbered time/standard tune
that she used to blank out the blame she felt bubble in
her in off times, an underground bilewater well that she
trained herself to answer before it could swell up to surface:
She hadn't left the boy with nothing—she'd left her son
with her lyrical genes and she'd made him a namesake of
musical meaning. She'd left her song with a song in his
heart so that he was ready and armed for the ravaging noise
of the world.

Cam reached toward her again; he was smiling this
time, his face slightly sanguine with effort. "I know what
you want," he said simply. "Und what's even better, I
know what you need." Lena dodged his caress, remem-
bering how she'd gritted her teeth at the start of this stint/

been willing to cash anything in, so she thought, for the
lure of a grip on her destiny. Her scheme for the dreamed
up-ahead was plotted with plans to provide what she needed
to ply her way forward. In the process she'd relieve herself
of deadweight freight like Minge Ames's mandate: *"Be
watchful what you ask for, lest you fool around an get it!"*

"I want you to be happy," Camvren had said without
frills on that formative day in K.C., the day they'd come
up with their plan to leave town together— "I want you to
be happy," he'd said, and she'd smiled. Though his expression was unchanged, he seemed to be pleased with her,
she could feel it— It seemed to her that her role in his
life could fill in the blank where his mirth and his color
should be.

"I want the best for you," Camvren was telling her.
"I'll make certain you haf what you need to do what it is
you're determined to do. I am a man of limited means"
(she knew differently yet she was patient) "but I'll do what
I can to how do you say?—I'll do what I can to put you
across."

Cam turned to her now, propping himself up on one
elbow. "Why don't we do this?" Supine like this with his
physique pressed into contouring bedsheets he called to
mind the new sculpture downstairs, an ivory figure by
Modigliani.

"Why don't we do what?" she wanted to know, and
she smiled, ready for anything, her beige body pressed
into contours of his milk-colored skin. She eased gleefully
into the four-poster's bedding; she'd felt welcoming comfort
like this only in silkridden dreams; now she was ready for
this sort of eiderdown bliss. Nine stories below were her

workaday elevators tugged to and vertical-fro on cords as
frayed as flayed talent. When she'd started work at the
hotel six months ago, she'd told herself that working the
cages was one way to get to the top. Time itself had proved
her true: here she was, and well hell, she was where she
belonged and had struggled to get.... Now the world of
waitpeople could wait.

"What is it you're thinking of?" She smiled at Cam's
look away into space. He lay on his back now, facing the
ceiling, his thewy legs spraddled with hers in between—
she'd already adjusted her body to his: *He's seeing his
future*, she thought. She wouldn't kid herself into thinking
he thought of romance; there was slim chance of that idle
theme in a mind like a map. One thing about Camvren,
he thought it through or bore with it whatever it was; Cam
was a diligent miner who panned through dregs of indicative
residue before he extracted its ore. He turned to face her
now with his look of completion—he'd come up with something, was laying it out to catch glints of the sun. "Harold
Muldoon," he said suddenly. "Do you vremember a Harold
Muldoon?"

Sure, she remembered Harry—how could she forget?
The oaf who ran the tobacco concession in the lobby right
next to her particular cage, stationed there by the devil
and sent to earth to do devilment.... She made certain
she kept herself out of his way. "Hi there, Miss Mighty"—
he'd grin when she came in—"You got any more-a that
poontang for Harry?" Yes, he said *"more,"* said it loud-
casual too, as if they'd been trimming for years— She
could have slow-choked that peckerwood, twisted his neck
with her wrists full of joy. He'd sidled up to her once on
the elevator, must have squeezed in when the cage had

been padded with passengers. She hadn't known he was there til she felt his breath on her neck and his hand on her hiney. "I know what you got for ole Harry," he drawled, flashing his Camels-stained raggedy teeth. "They tell me you gals is a blip in the sack," he said then with the same gruesome grin. She quickturned to face him, greeting his balls with the bone of her knee. He dropped to address his condition and heard her say clearly, "They shoulda tole yew thuh end a thuh story." She let her speech slide into the redneck's own twang. "We so wild an woolly— Colored gals is fulla spunk too." She wrenched the el dial with one hand behind her, keeping her eyes on the dog while they lurched downward toward the ground floor with its well-could-be hell. She knew this full well: If it wasn't for Cam in her life—Cam the blond bossman with star-spangled sayso—certainty was, she'd be fired on the spot. Yes, she remembered Harry, like a bad time from a chronic disease.

"I've thought of something thad shood be good fun." Camvren was cupping her breast with one hand, licking its nipple with his stiffpointed tongue. He tilted his head in order to focus on her. "I'll wager we make an interesting picture." He worked one leg roughly on top of hers. "Don't you think so? But . . . my dear Lena, the sing-gher," he said with a flourish, "performance is everything. You know as well as I do, the best shows begin with a goot strong tableau."

She waited, looking into his eyes.

"There's one thing we lack."

She showed surprise, knew a cue when it came.

"What's the one thing we're missing? I'll grant you guess."

She shook her head, patient.

"All right, I will tell you. It iss the audience that we require. This worker, this Hairee, he wants to watch us when we perform, just like this. I know," he said to her shock, "he is a dolt. Such an idiot. He iss a harmless dunderhead though."

She jumped to her feet. *Watch your words,* an inner voice told her. "I, I . . . ," she heard herself stammer, "I couldn't do that."

"Don't be silly," Cam said. He'd flushed red from some force of effort, a secreted strain. How she must've looked! she thought later—it must have been the way that she looked that brought about his adroit turnaround. "As you wish," he said with a dismiss-it shrug. "We will wait until you half reached your maturity in physical matters. You *kinderschwarzen* are just like the rest of your countrymen, childish in such things as this."

Like the rest of your countrymen. . . . This is what found itself filed in her mind: Cam compared her to whites on an openfaced basis, nevermind race hate or dutiful prejudice and nevermind abolitionists' bleached point of view, here was a white man who treated her humanly, so she thought then in the days when she told herself she'd put up with his ways . . . at least until days of near dreamed up Ahead. So she'd packed her belongings, including the weight of her witsmatch with Meech and her guilt about the boy: *I'll do what I know I was put on the planet for— That's good for me and for all else concerned—* She'd determined to dogtail her destiny wherever it took her, and she smiled with mild strain when she thought of the baby she'd named for the path of her dreams: She'd wind up, she knew, in nearby Chicago with its doughflow nightclubs still the hub of everyday life in the wake of its patron, dilute Prohibition. She'd sing her way clear to wherever fate took her, it was her duty, she had to break free.

She'd named the boy Chicago so as to give him the best of herself, and the best of herself was her future. She wanted to bless him with all the grace she could come up with and what she came up with was soon and not now, there and not here in K.C. Missouri, where dreams you cast forward boomeranged back so that you ducked or were wounded by shrapnel of impossibility. In her typical manner, she strove for what was just out of reach—the city Chicago, that race-record base where women like her were making their mark on the Jim Crow–controlled industry. So much for Sophie's would-be-black blues, brash Bessie Smith had popped open the top of wax disc recording and Alberta Hunter had taken the stage. Blues and jazz divas were broaching the forefront with songs of their own full of brass-tacks opinion, female opinion on how things were stacked and how to unstack them . . .

> *You better pull yourself togethuh*
> *And start actin wild*
> *Cuz wild women*
> *Don't have the blues!*

Then she'd come back and take the boy with her to where a black man could grow without feeling slow death in his muscles, the limp slack of atrophied chance. She'd go to a place full of new opportunity, a place full of fortune too raw and uncertain for skin-color folly: The name of her dream was Chicago.

Then came Cam with his easy-route offer for her to

debut in his new cabaret in far Montevideo, a place that pockmarked the map of potential eroded by race-hate America and beckoning Europe-based war. It was the fall of mid-'30 when they arrived in that corner of heaven to stay at the Villa la Playa until Cam's Hotel Björn's construction was finished, monument to magic of means that it was with its outlook through pale stucco archways that stretched above Río de la Plata's steep cliffs below. To the south was the government palace decked in deals for repasts that the Western world craved—*café* that aroused and *cacao* that kindled in so many ways.

The heat of the region had militant presence—it rose from the noonday promenade in visible takeover waves/ demanded *siesta* as tribute to torpor/filled you with languorous fluid that oozed through the body as sensuous glue. Sun seeped into skin in thin redolent rays, melting the mind into focus on flesh. . . . Cam had started his "play-scenes" in no time, as soon as they'd arrived, it seemed. He'd set out on foot for the Moor-built cathedral when the structure was outlined by spotlighting moonlight ("to study the architecture," he said, "I can contemplate there"); or to the *cabildo* ("for respite," he said) and then "Do you object?"—his signal for her to leave him alone.

Just turn down the volume of loud shouting doubt: she told herself this though she knew what the evidence pull-clued her to; she'd seen Cam's involvement with women who pleased him by bearing their beauty, long-stemmed tropical blossoms with roots raised to view, black-haired *morenas* who moved with heads lifted aloft bearing marketgoods baskets as crowns. She knew his yen for the sway of brightly inviting, full-skirted hips/felt his senses that savored raw honey to be. The women he chose were

all to the count far darker than she was, *negritas* he sought
with a thirst for the color he needed to feed him somehow.

"*Do you object?*"

She'd agreed with herself to keep silent for sake of
her access to sources she needed, it was simple as that,
though she'd told herself in the course of her transit from
home to new home when her growing-up years were a
certainless string of improbable promises from play fathers
and unlikely fostering "uncles": *Maybe I'm an outside
child, but I'll never be an outside woman. . . .* Yet she'd let
herself down in a manner that couldn't be mended. She'd
done things for Camvren that haunted her sense of due toll
for love, though this thing they were in wasn't that and she
knew it, so rules of behavior were few and flayed open—
even brand-new they'd been frayed at the seams. She'd
told herself that she'd never take part in the "games" Cam
produced, she never would play in the sexual dramas he
staged; yet she'd been the star of more than one scene that
still riddled recall. . . .

It was after midnight when she heard double footsteps
on the tiled passage that led to her offset salon—one set
of steps the tentative taps of a woman's high heels.

". . . but what can we do? We are required to enjoy
life," she heard Camvren say with his short mirthless
laugh.

Contralto response filtered upward. "*Sí, pero no so-
lamente este.* We are required to be careful." They laughed.

With shutters aside, she could see the deep secret
blue of night sky where a lone macaw circled in cyclic
confusion, punctuating the stillness with bold warbled
calls. The dome-shaped gate of the villa glistened in dark

leaves of trees set against distance that narrowed, a furcated wedge to forever. She felt fate stretch backward to guide her . . . she knew what lay in the near-nexus "future." When they reached her room she was ready/already had made her decision: She would "play" as Cam wanted and refuse to be bruised by her role in his rich-tempered skits; she would adapt to his heat-seeking ways.

Lodestar Codas,

Woodwind Modes

L E N A
M o n t e v i d e o , 1 9 3 3

| *I let a song go out of my heart*— That's how I feel
about the boy, almost called him a baby—no use starting
that ill-suited jive, not even in childhood, much less on
into life like some mothers drag it to foolsgild themselves
against roughhewn truth with its sharp-edged slag: Black
men don't get to be boys. I face my facts and their fangs—
   "Well. Do tell." She heard the old voice in her head.
   I love that child more than dear life itself!
   "You coulda fooled me."
   I can't take it sometimes; the guilt weighs me down.
The guilt and some sort of challenge, unruly and too tough
to master. *"You come from a long line of genius-ass niggers.
Put that book down!"* Minge Ames's voice rang in her head.
*"You got more to learn from listenin to me than from what
any white scribbler can tell you!"* She pictured the family

reunions, loud-shouting monolog sessions where newly known uncles would rant at the top of their lungs, point to themselves and their stopped-up magnificence, hard-muscled brilliance chained to the gate. *"A man like me is too much for these crackers,"* old Uncle Zeke would be yelling, finger to chest. *"These puny-minded fools fear me, that's what. And you see*—he leaned toward her small up-turned face to share whiskey-warm breath—*"THAT'S WHY THEY DO ME LIKE THEY DO."* He'd been nineteen when he came out of Kansas State University with that dead-end degree he never could use, and brother, believe me, he'd paid his tall dues. He'd been the only colored on campus, day after day til sundown that is, when law had him hotfoot to where he "belonged," in the part of town roped off for him and his kind. But he wasn't roped off in his mind, that's what riddled him so like it riddled her now: the slave breaker's bridle always surprised him as it did her and the rest of the Ameses. It caught them off guard that their dreams and ambitions could be fenced in, then saddled and ridden by other folks, white or tamed colored. That shackle was what she intended to see to it never got to her lone son Chicago, not while he was young so it stunted his growth—but low-minded Meech had thought different.

"You think you can frill up his life just to suit im? A man's gotta be a man. . . ."
"Meaning what?"
"Woman, you hear me ast you anythang?"
She shook her head, numb. She remembered how he'd been in the days of their courting, short-spoken, anxious to please, then had turned caustic and hellbent with bile like an overgrinned untethered slave.

"You oughta know what it takes to be a man—you spend time enough tryin to climb into make-believe britches. Mark my word: Any headbump this halfgirl sissy come up against, thass jest the headbump he need. He too soft as is—look at im hummin to hisself lak a limp-wristy girl, whisperin to hisself all hunched down in a goddamn corner—he done already turned do-funny or addlebrain, one. . . ."

It was how she'd gone on to give in to the press of her dream so that she'd been willing to give the boy up to somebody like Meech, a tack that pierced through to the secret-thin skin of her need to succeed *through* to something, to make her worthwhile to herself—it was that choice that grated her so. Still and all, Meech was a rover; she thought he'd provide other mothers for 'Go. How could she know what Meecham was willing to do just to spite her?

"He whipped me, Mamsy, with the ironin cord." No sooner had she told 'Go who she was that day at the malt shop then all Hades erupted and flame-wreathed her in. Motherhood was a role she'd thought she'd slip into, she'd re-don the thing like an old pair of shoes. But her feet were reshaped by time's cobblestone edgeways: bunions and calluses had formed. Yet the moment he'd known who she was, 'Go had been eager to claim her as mother with no reservation: "I'll call you 'Mamsy,'" he said.

She gripped his wrists lying listless on the table between them. Laughter swirled up all around them, seeming to mock any show of raw earnestness. The boy's sudden sharing brought tears to her eyes. "Are you saying Meech brutalized you? How many times did he— When did he— What brought it on? *Are you hurt?*"

Meech approached the boy man to man, slamming into his surprise with both fists. So the tyke thought he was good, did he? Thought he was quick enough to outslick his pap . . . . He want to be mannish? Waal, the right time is now. The boy covered his head from the blows as best as he could; he was caught off guard, snatched out of free-falling dreams into a gust of Pap's wrath. The attack had taken him by surprise this time cause 'Go had been deep in the soft wheezing sound of his horn. He'd finally breathed into the sax—how could he resist—just enough to send a thin stream of pressure-packed wind into the mouthpiece. . . . He hadn't even heard Pap's flatfooted foray into the zone 'Go'd thought was home safe.

"Thought I tole yuh tuh turn that horn in." Meech marked the beat of the words with his fists. His assault took on a sickly rhythm that had curious appeal for the boy. *"Didn't . . . I tell . . . yuh? You think I'm a fool?"*

'Go's dodging the blows incensed the man further; he stepped up the pace of his jabs, managing now to swipe the tyke's snooty-bridged nose with the jags of his scar-thickened knuckles. If the whitetime whelp thought he could bamboozle Cyrus T. Meecham, well now was the time he'd learn different.

No sooner had Meech and the boy moved back yonder, down South, where according to Meech "leastways a nig knows exact where he stands," then the horn had come packaged in brown wrapping paper, signed with no name and with no note of origin, other than "Overseas Airmail" said over again in two or three languages not quite the same, at least so it seemed to the boy: he'd learned how to figure things out for himself. The address on the label was messy, marked "Forward" in what looked to be pen-

script in more than one hand. . . . Meech was on 'Go's
heels the minute the mystery arrived at the door in the
form of a tornpaper note from old Colter Sloan, who owned
the store and general-delivery post there inside it. "Come
to git chore packitge from hell?" the grizzled old man had
guffawed when he and Pap made their way to the worn
wooden counter, heads bent, caps in hand in riddled respect for the redneck behind it. *"Must* be from hell," the
cracker crowed loud to the crowd of do-nothing 'necks who
lounged in the store. "I say *must* be from hell . . . cuz here
cums two black devils ta git it!"

'Go still heard their hooted guffaws once he was home
and sure-ready to open the box clearly made out to him,
so said the red-and-black label. . . . In a streak of wild
luck, Pop had let him carry the oddly shaped parcel all
the way down the road to their home, telling the boy, "You
the one to tote this. Got yo' mark on it, ain't it? Whoever
it name mean he the mule." Pop made himself laugh in
the fumes of the store episode. *Goddamn crackers: black
man's bane. . . .* Swallerin they gaff made him wanna . . .
He cuffed the boy hard across the head just to think of it.
"Whatchew lookin at? You don't like whatchew see?" He
took a swig from his flask and guzzled it hard as they made
their way forward, him in the head, the boy ten even paces
behind him just like Meech trained him. *High yella addlebrain whelp, like a pale-headed haint sent to dog him,
to nip at his heels an to feed off the juice from his nerves. . . .*

It was when they were back at what Pap called "the
barn" that 'Go had hunched over his bundle ready to tug
loose its ties. Pap grabbed the box from him. "Anythang
come into *this* corner a earth belong first an only to me.
Case you don't know it, I'm the one keep your soul an

scraggly body half stuck together as they is. I bring the bread into this home, joke that it is. An you? Look at you. You couldn't help a lame bitch over a stile. I know an you know, in this doghole you don't lend a hand to jack doodley." Meech snatched the box from the boy and started to budge its frayed string. Things as they was, he'd be the one to free its rash mystery.

Then's when the package seemed to take life of its own, seeming to be as bent as was Meech to release its hidden insides. As if by conjure a long mojo horn clattered to the floor; it was gleam-happy gold and wore knobby pearl buttons down the lank of its neck to where a round funnel belled out with a secretive flare. 'Go was dazed by the instrument's promise, so caught off guard he was moved to a loud burst of laughs that trailed in a screech, vexing openmouthed Meech beyond tolerance. It seemed like a dream: Papa startled one instant, the next instant grabbing toward 'Go, snatching the tyke by the front of his collar Pap twisted in one fed-up fist. Pap's veins were distended; he looked like he'd lost track of reason, just beating the boy, cuffing him first on one side of his prime-suspect head. He always was suspect . . . then's when it started, the series of bent-intent beatings that burst into being like spontime combust, Papa's lightening attacks when 'Go least knew they were coming/was clueless to what set them off, dull-witted whelp that he was as Pap told him: "Yuh got no-good in yuh deep to the bone, ain't worth the spasm that birthed yuh."

What got to Meech damnmore than all else was the Phantom's desertion, disloyal bitch that she was, no not bitch, if anything she weren't rightly that—what she'd been was his redeemin dream: truth told to none but his sniggerin self sneerin at high hopes grown willful like weeds gone to seed away up past fences of practical need. When he met her he'd thought he hadn't a haint of a chance, but she'd beckoned him to her an like a dumb kickme dog he'd rushed in; that was the last lasso that wore him so thin.

He blasted his breath out fast-hot through his nostrils in order to make himself tarry. *Shoved aside—he'd been shoved aside from his factory post right after the war when the doughboys came back, Euro doughboys an their counterpart cousins steamshipped to these shores in chalk-colored droves. . . . He'd been recruited at first, right fore they'd fought that there moneyman's war— Henry Ford an Bessemer an alla their like had sent out their scouts way down South just to snare somesuch Negroes as him for their mills an their foundries, grinding blast hot as they all were back then, thanks to black Garrett P. Morgan, the man who'd invented self-lubrication so that all the machines no longer shut down; they hum-ground gears flexed with juice that fed axles an grindstones an cogs just like him an his kind, just long enough for a free-dreamin nightmare turned while. When he lost his job to the welcomebacked paddies, that's when he'd turned an gone home from the fire to the fryinpan South.*

Lena'd known Meech was sick with self-rankling that drove him to temper, yet she hadn't suspected the depth of his rage. To Lena in hindsight it seemed that her part in 'Go's pain stood out clearly in sun-silhouette, backlit by her own default. When she'd sent 'Go the saxophone, she'd been fed up with Camvren and Montevideo . . . she'd come across the small horn in the band's dressing room one night before her show in the hotel casino, and she'd thought instantly of young Chicago back home; she didn't know why—the boy was only nine by now and'd never shown serious sign of a musical knack to her knowledge before she'd had to leave home. What drew her to the horn for the boy was its beauty—the curlicues etched in a welcoming well that wended its way to a clear-passage bell. The instrument seemed set to proclaim its own beauty inside and out without doubt of its duty to be as it was, an exquisite musical conduit ready to liven the life-love of all who would hear it. She'd bought the sax for a song from its owner who rarely used it; he was drawn to raspy-toned saxophone tenor and the deep-throated voice of low baritone. As for Camvren, he'd laughed with the joy of loose spirit when he'd seen what it was that she'd bought.

"Now I know you ere mad," he'd said with a grin at men's folly including her starring role in it. "What is it you've bought with this gift that iss at heart for yourself? Half you bought your reprieve? What sound does amnesty make?" He took her hand and swung it in synchronized swing with his own. "Come, you tell me," he urged with a wink. "You can tell me. What key is it in?"

It came to her then what she'd known all along: Cam was a first-order diagnostician. His specialty? Other folks' scabbed-over ills that he peeled to expose the soft underflesh pulsing hidden below. She'd grown sick of his routine exams that always provoked her own bitter findings and realization that probing for illness was part of the sickness itself. . . .

"*Now I know where to come for my bromide. . . .*" She'd gone on to do what Cam wanted, set aside her sense of herself to get her work done. As for moral misgivings, she'd made a date with herself on the far side of life to reckon with those; she'd take note of woebegones now and net them further along in the future if need be. It was senseless to weigh herself down with topheavy rules when all else in the thirties was flux and ripe flexibility— It was time she loosed the bindings she'd used to gird herself with back in heretofore life as a self-guarded child. For reality's sake she'd gone on to do Harry Muldoon and all the follow-up Harrys, and she fought with herself after each of her roles in Cam's playscenes. She still was distressed by her new self vamped up to order at the same time she suffered from what she could be.

El Hotel Björn was completed three years after they'd come, its construction derailed by overdue shipments of goods from *América norte* caught fast in the yaw of the Crash. She'd made her casino debut four months later, wearing her fuchsia gown of *crepe de chine*, singing *"I Let a Song Go Out of My Heart"* to a housefull crowd of entrepreneurs with their pastime *señoritas*—she torched the sultry atmosphere/scorched the thoughtwraps away from pulsating feelings. The show was an omen of great things to come, she'd thought then. Camvren had joined in her dream though with schemes of his own.

"I haf big plans for you," he said later that night in their room. "I haf plans for you and yet you indulge yourself in a show of naïveté." He stood so that they no longer faced each other. "It takes a *primitif* to deprecate the difference between sport and the duties of life. Think what it is that I ask of you."

"And the hell with my feelings of course."

He reddened in silence. "There is no feeling involved," he said finally, serving the words in slowmeasured

drams. "The only feeling involved is there on that bed."
He turned his face toward her; she read its corrective
appraisal. "The man is a business associate, nothing more.
He has seen you on stage and he fancies you. You are to
respond to his interest. What is it that you don't understand?"

"You expect me to whore til you call it quits." She
said the thought as a statement; it seemed as fantasy, their
keen worlds-apartness when the globe had been joined by
vast shared machine.

He kicked the chair where he stood. "Why will you
complicate what is a game? We are big boys and girls.
Half you noticed?" His lips were compressed in a multi-
rayed crease for the interval when he disallowed himself
to speak. When he resumed, it was as if he were parsing
the words. "I do not see how I can continue to feature you
in the cabana when you are not ready to comport yourself
as a woman." By the time she reached toward him, he had
stepped back.

'Go told her later, he'd never forget; it came to mind
unbidden that day in the malt shop, sharp-tanged with
intolerable truth. He'd run away that day in '33 when he
was thirteen, 'Go had said. . . .

*We were still livin in 'sippi where Pap's mam had died
an left him her property such as it was. Pap had stropped
me again, this time for my birthday—twelve hard licks an
a thirteenth one "to grow on." He'd lend me what life had
in store, so he said. I don't know what it was that rose,
rared up in me; I was used to regard that Pap let me feel
and I'd already devised my own fit-me response: I'd just
blow silent notes on my horn til I could manage to hear the*

*song it was singin, or if Pap let me out, I'd shout screech-
hollow notes through my horn that made birds in the woods
take to wing. That particular day, when I got to the clearing,
I realized I'd had it, I'd have to cut out, I was damn nigh
a man an overdue ready for change, so I set out to seek it.
It wasn't til dark fell that I found it, in form of three
marksmen armed at the ready an set to hunt coon. They
was laughin an guzzlin their 'shine when I was slipshod
enough to let em hear me an my loudtalkin horn.*

*"Well, what we got heah?" said a thick cracker, wrin-
kled and burnt red by sun.*

*"Look like a swamp rat, you ast me," the second 'neck
said.*

*The third shook his stringy-haired head. "Looky,
looky," he said.*

*I was standin stock-still, couldn't make myself take off
like I shoulda done long ago, way fore they caught me.
Niggers an woods mutts were one when it came to knowin
to run long fore danger appeared close at hand. We knew
not to let it creep up, close in near. . . .*

"Whutzat he's tootin? Don't sound lak no juice harp."

*"One way to see," the red-colored crack said. "Boy,
come on up here." He showed a tobacco-y grin aimed at
me all while—I could see this; they never give credit or
care—while he side-mouthed to the greasy-head 'neck,
"Close in on 'im quick, fore he breaks yonder." They
snatched my horn from me in no time— "Whut kinda tune-
turn is this?" A peckerwood grabbed at me—when he'd
craned sideways to see I saw somethin too: what might be
my last chance to break free, but I couldn't bear to tear
away cuz I couldn't bear to give up my horn, self-silly kid
that I was, same as this boy you see standin here now. It*

*was what they did next that managed to make me cut loose:
The first cracker put my ax to his lips an blew til he turned
purple 'thout bringin out nary a sound. His ole boys were
grinnin an skinnin, markin his pains til he tired of the strain
an whirled around all of a sudden, holdin my horn overhead. Then he did what I dreaded, let my horn fly, into a
mossywood tree. When the other two 'necks were bustin a
gut—one gave a loud rebel yell—I made my break, straight
back to Pap's by a mite after midnight. He was up waitin,
bidin his time, all set to welcome me home in the usual way
so he thought, mindless of how I'd cut out for K.C. before
sunrise could catch up with me.*

It was for Cam and his schemes she'd left young
Chicago? She was plagued by her own ruthless hindsight
and had to admit what appeared to her view: She'd have
to leave here, to get back to 'Go if he'd have her. It was
'38 when she'd come to that chosen solution after Owens
strode blackly through the Olympics, the year Joe Louis
was slammed back into place by transient teutonic hope.
Now she found that she wasn't absolved even yet from her
folly. . . . She wasn't reprieved by herself in the absence
of fame she thought would sure-cure her; what took its
place was parasite guilt that soaked up the dregs of her
energy. What was the use? She'd fooled herself for too long
as it was. She wondered at times if she'd made herself fail.

*I've been no better than Meech in the way I've treated
the boy*— It was this she considered in moments of ego-
free clarity. She had to be true, and to face facts as they
were; she'd learned early on to regard herself with less
slack than she'd leave in her view of another. She was
partial to brash glaring truth due to her birthsign, the

scales, Minge told her the day that she met her. Whatever its source, *balance* remained uppermost in her mind, and a dullard could see she was out of whack in the wake of her leaving the boy unbalanced as she was and singing his own likely off-notes out of tune to life's key.

I let a song go out of my heart. . . . She'd left the boy with no buffer to brace his dreams up against, no guard-fence between his soft heart and Meech's mistreatment, though she hadn't known— *But I should have!*—the reach of Cyrus's meanness, that it would stretch straight through to Chicago, harmless and separate from her as he was. To wound the boy further—what did it matter, by fault or by folly?—she'd ballcut the boy by leaving him saddled with her sensitivity, a legacy suited for ruling-class girls. In her self-lighted focus of earlier years, she'd been as dim-sighted as Meech. 'Go would be a young teen now and she'd have to leave Cam to seek her reprieve. She'd go back to the States in order to locate the boy.

MODE three

Consummate Noise &

Those Gotta-Have

Boys

K A T
S a n   F r a n c i s c o ,   1 9 9 0

It was winter at the time of both rounds of my dream
in the spiral of Lena with Camvren, and Kitty with Meech-
spawned Chicago—a turgid time when I'm suffused with
helplessicity, the cataplexed feeling of watching myself as
dumbfounded caught-off-guard dreamer charmed into gen-
erative slumber. I wanted to shake myself awake . . . to
swing suddenly to the right of my dream and plant my feet
with resolution on sane-sapling floorboards of Now. Yet
these visions from heretofore fascinate me! They could be
mere offshoots of my stopped creativity (or so I said at that
time when I'd failed to compose yet and still at poor Plexus).
The images I see in interior life could be only a scheme
of my creative source enabling me to gather loose fruits of
the muse and then say To hell with the tree, it's of no mind
to me. . . . I stubbed the big toe of my mind on this thought

and couldn't go further past knowing, *It's my own inner clime that catapults me through time*: away from the drift of day-to-day life with its creative-void type of strife, toward bygone times of grace and face-saving, of okay delay. I was called to the set of my ongoing characters (especially the character Kitty, about whom I thought, *Between her and me there's more than ID; she's a woman like I am, in search of her own need to be. Who are we to resist deep-rooted destiny?*) So what's the harm in my transits to past? They're just something to do when I'm blue. This little mindplay's my favorite quirk, a mild palliative at the edge of berserk. . . .

I'd fired Vide by now from my life, and Karl'd made his Exit Stage Left, all of which left me bereft with neither half of my lovelorn equation, only dismal zero and nothing to add up to but what *I* bring to bear, an unknown quantity; *X* equals me. When Vide made his break, C.T. had been working his way through labyrinth keys, Cecil Percival Taylor, C.P.T., who's knightlike-undaunted/dubbed with his own sense of timing and circumspect rhymings of rhythm— His only holdback is late-again critics flapping, dry-rapping like yesterday's leaves on his heels as he trudges through forest of lone-spirit avant garde gloom— Life: It's a solo of crink-tinkling keys on their own with a prehensile hook to the past that nobody can see— Just ask Cecil. Ask me!

In the course of my city safari, studies in search of the real, I was there in the train station that day, headed for Berkeley where life and times are free as a bee (or insinuate such in good grace), and Berkeley, it's brimming with creative *stim*, so I knew I'd settle for any place I ended up over there in that nook of the East Bay where anything's

fair . . . visible madness lays itself open for all to partake
of, to share. That's why I'd hied me to Bay Area Rapid
Transit (*B.A.R.T.*, speed-craving natives would say) where
I stood now, nonchalant and pretending-directed by inner
staunch-centered self, under neon sign "CONCORD! CON-
CORD! CONCORD!" flashing its warning: Train coming! (And
watch out, all you dark folks, you might be bound for the
east knell of hell where that last one of you was lynched
only fourscore or so days ago, and not in your integral
dreams but in corporeal B.A.R.T. station instead, late one
allwhite night.)

Around me were standing the usuals poised in sce-
nario: a passel of casual greys—they called em "ofays'"
back in the forties—one standing haphazard hip in fly
dungarees reinforced with fashionable tears at the knees
and more ports of entry designed to please free open spirits
like me . . . dig how he wears hair razor-razed on both sides,
leading to wisps of formative boxcut fenced in a square by
cowlicky straight-geléed standing-up strands. Speaking of
which, here in San Flan with its influx of Chingoes and
yen-happy Japs, here in San Span where the Black factor's
slack, do ya dig how the amber among us, influx of Asians
en masse, master that *In* to the bank in flash no-time, it's
true, regardless of prejudged or slanted-type view of anti-
admirers like me who can't seem to click with their *oeuvre*
or its groove in reference to rhythmic impulse; we've got
a beat warp between us, black race and yellow—something
to do with how we prize outward expression, improvaneity.
Nevertheless though and regardless—let's bring this rap
down to tacks, just the facts ma'am of your cravenmost
subjective view—I do understand and do dig the young

unuptight ones with their technostyle fashion, their robot
raked hair. . . .

Then, looka there, down near the dark where Concord
track merges with seeming nowhere, there in the gloom
with its Doppler effect of horn of a ghost train that sounds
its way forward with deflated bellow belching through distance that swells— Down there's two bruthas in dreads
and with whitegirl decor close at hand, never far, tight as
knaps on a lamb. *White thiiighs.* . . . The scene puts me in
mind of that rap of Last Poets; remember the bittersweet
citreous jam called "White Thighs"?—citric spoof prick-
ling consciousness buds in the sixties when puckers of
morals were outwardly tanged and perused with sharp zest.
"OOOH, white thighs!" the riff went— Don't get me started
re rastas and studfinder whitegirls, the latter in hunt and
former in militant quest of the snare: (*"Shuh mon, eye don'
see nutting wrong wid it. Dese gulls, dey got to be serviced
by* some*buddy. Ain't it so now?"*)

I know how it goes, pick up the rapped rationale in
my mystified mind (*Somethin old, somethin new. . . . Rasta
Mon Meets Cindy Lou*) when two coy boys slip by, one of
them suited in Swede-Euro collarless shirt made of muslin,
the other in loose freeform slacks of *no matter to us what
you latecomers think*—these hitting at ankles in ManRay
print sox— The s/he/s nod and signal pursed lips to each
other on flit between recounts of wit, snits, and aeries.

". . . okay," says one to the other. "Name the dwarfs
and we'll see."

"That's easy," s/he answered. "First there was
Sleepy. . . ."

"I'm impressed," said the other.

"Then there was *Wheezy*...."

"Right. That makes two."

"Next was *Nasty*...."

"And *Mopey*...."

"Gropey...."

"... and *Nutty*.... How many've we got?"

"Two to go. The sixth was *Rebutty*...."

"He was my favorite."

"And then there was *Sleazy*—he's number seven."

"He was that nice sex-change dwarf, don't you remember?"

"But of course, dear; how could I forget?"

Then's when two elder blackwomen pass at a clip of their own, both of them from the South, you could tell, (*Hush yo' mouth* !), both of them sturdy, planting feet firmly on subway concrete, pushing their shopcarts, tall vertical vessels of fenced-in groceries and such—they push them in tandem, leaning on crossbar handles awhile til each woman musters her breath and it's time to push resolute-forward, using the pushcarts as mobilized canes.

From them I'd picked up a snatch of amazing i-change, after which I was forced to come to and scramble so as to eavesdrop on sly as they started to talk yet again.

"Girl, you better get you some a that beef brisket from Safeways whilst it still on sale."

"How much it goin for?"

"They got it up there for a dollar ninety-nine cent a pound—"

"That ain't bad, considerin."

"Sho' you right. Things be so high nowdays."

"Includin the peoples sellin it to you, I *swear*."

"*Girl*. I know what you mean."

"Sometime I be done gone for a good solid week 'thout seein nobody sober but me."

"You better know it."

"Make you question your sense. Am I gettin lightheaded or what?"

"Naw, it's the whorl. The whole damn whorl is got high as a kite on the first day a March."

"Ain't it so though? An these *kids*, stayin hopped up on this new dope they done made just to keep em like slaves—"

"Drugs do em so they don't know they butt from they forehead."

"Lord, *Lord*. That's what I cain't reckon."

"Don't let it gitjo pressure up. Give it up to the Lord. *He'll* make a way."

"But when? Seem like He a day late an a dollar short, you ask me."

"Watch yo mouf now. Don't try ta sass Him. You know like I do, He'll have the last word."

"Yeah, well I'll tell you the truth: I don't hear Him talkin, not to these monkey-mind kids out here. Am I wrong? You think on it. Don't mean to blasphemy so 'scuze if I spoke outa turn, but like I say, Addie, you know me. I be thinkin alla time—"

"You hadn't oughta trouble yo'seff so. Don't let life *work* you."

"I thank you for yo' concern, but the puddin done already set. Old as I is, I cain't help bein me. I be thinking things *through*."

I do too, and I'm floating their words in my memory tank as I'm ogling the world in the subway like this, just trying to bop to my rockbeat *Lookatthat!* groove when up pops who else but Chloe with her bright blatant self; I'd called her to see if she'd come down to meet me, and she'd agreed to do so "after I go pay my talk bill," she said, so I'd braced for what could be a vigil onwending in apt c.p.t.; I'd packed my provisions: more tape food for Nexus, my Walkman— Nexus and me, we know how to wait and make waits worthwhile. I'd just flipped the switch so that Cecil'd begun to wend in from the bend of where music imps meet, flash Cecil T captured on wax in Dark Forest of Germany, nevermind aryan superiority dream, CT'd brought his own scheme of brash get-to-this! brilliance, a tune he must've first heard in hermetic elliptical craters of moon; he called the tune "Dark to Themselves" and here worked it through bold Bosendorfer piano's eight extra keys, *schriiing sprechen zee pling!* flanked all the while by his passel of negritude gnomes, namely Lyons, Parker, and rash bad Bakir— Caught in their fury I'm whirled up in formative tornado funnel when earthly impulse takes leave to tug at my sleeve and I see that beside me is Chloe.

"Hey girl, what it be like? Thought I'd never make it. Honey, let me tell you," Chloe broke off. She was dressed in some sort of smock that was speckled with paint selected, she said, for mood/to adjust her down attitude. "I couldn't find the string of my new IUD. When I felt up inside me the damn thing was lost, it musta been missin in action I thought; scared me damn nigh to death when I thoughta the way I'd been screwin, havin the time of my life cuz I thought I was free— Are you listenin to me?"

I turned Cecil down to a roar. "Talk to me."

"Fore I had this thang put in, I was hangin my hopes on that foam—"

"Lucky Whip. That won't get it—"

"You think I don't know? Contraceptive foam, an that mess of a gel—"

"Yeah, well what can I tell you? All the above takes the oomph out of love."

She made her eyes wide. "But what's a young whore to do?"

We fell out in rash laughs like we're wont to do, we dark few sandwiched into the rest's imaged grimace, but let me hop back on track: When she bent toward me in mirth, I could see strands of gilt twine Chloe'd threaded through her blond 'locks, making her head glow in a halo of weird luminosity.

"No joke though," she threw in when we'd surfaced for air, "what kinda control do *you* use?"

"All I can get since the AIDS plague afflicteth all o'er the land."

"Preach, sistergirl." She looked off for an instant in dream. " 'Member when times was so level we could fuck free?"

"Don't start my nostalgia, I recall it so well: I had two lovers, they each had two too—"

"Yeah, well now that's taboo—"

"For all but the risky—"

"For all but the fools."

"Seems like a fable. Time was, sex was simple. Just last summer the livin was easy. . . ." I sang the rest: *"Fish was jump-pin . . . an the cotton was hi-igh. . . ."*

We were two giggling loons when the train stopped beside us, a fugitive banshee from bleak underpass of chilly-gloom air. Two blackkids stepped out, damnear on us at that with no note of our presence or boarding intent, being bent as they were to their boombox blasting *"no matter what the name/we're all the same/PIECES/in one big chess game/Poets Supreme/We nuke for truth/bazooka the scheme!"*—"Don't Believe the Hype" by rapsatirical chorus in spades dubbing itself *Public Enemy: Don't laugh a minute/We're rap stranglers/you can't angle us/I know you're listenin/I caught yuh pissin/yuh pants. . . ."*

"Cut it up, Slice!" Chloe calls out, but the boyz (*Bring the noise!*)—the boyz are enrap/tured so pay her no mind, and I dig how she walks as we ease toward the B.A.R.T. train's last empty seat. She seems sorta slumped, somehow bowed in a way. By the time we sit she's grown silent and I notice her pallor in now-lit fluorescence, leading me forthwith to say, "How you feel really?" No doubt about it, her mood's shifted as mine do in the wink of a split-second blink. I look at her closely, see dark wary circles hung under her sloe hazel eyes, and so lighten my asking with the flip of a tease. "You ain't lookin so rippty dippty. Talk to me, girl."

It took her a while to bounce back. "I don't know." She said the words slowly, seeming to search fargone depths of herself. "Sometime I be *down*, seem like all of a sudden." She sighed. "You can't win for losin. Know what I mean?"

"Like a champ." I led her to mash out the rest.

"It's these *men* we got goin."

"I shoulda known." Chloe'd spoken of some sort of set-to with Sadiq, a riff that had gone down just days before, so in the spirit of Whew! *Ain't we glad that all's said and done*, I decided to bring up their previous tiff. "What's this about Sadiq buggin your headspace though?" I asked Chloe.

"What?" she said, almost to herself. "Oh. That ain't Sadiq, it's Kamau I was talkin about." A frown creased her forehead and furrowed her brow.

"What's he up to now?"

"Bein demandin." She shook her head once with spent patience. "Bein Kamau."

I made myself wait; I was humming the head of "New Boogie For Thoughtful Woogies," a themepiece composed by my wildgenius pal name of lean Leonard King.

"We'd be makin the rounds of the galleries," Chloe threw down. "We was at Samuel's in Jack London Square yesterday an he was bein damn disagreeable—I shined him on the best that I could. You say the sky is blue . . . 'Naw, it's chartreuse,' he'd say."

"He's Scorpio, right?"

"With assinity risin." Chloe was bitter, saying her say in a tart sort of way. "I just told im, 'Look, honey,' I said, 'I'm temperamental my*self*, so don't be bringin that temper to *me*, man. I got my own.'"

"And you're runnin on Full with your own gas alone."

She flared for a moment, then simmered down sitting stiffly erect as if something riddled her spine. "Beg pardon?" she said with attempted small smile. I could see Kamau now with his goingoff self, tall six feet five and so fine he still looked sublime even when snapped out of whack, when life in the black had wrenched him off track of his painterly calling for which he was sent to the planet. . . .

"I got a lot a men callin me," Chloe was saying with

would-be smug comfort, "more than my share, to hear
people tell it, which is a wonder, the way that I treat em."
She stopped to grin. "That's the trick of it maybe—just
treat em bad. 'Course you can't keep em that way. But I'll
tell you what. The ones I don't have is the ones I don't
need all wrapped up round my neck—"

"And your art—"

"They require too much care an feedin. Hell, I ain't
even got no houseplants that need constant care. I stick
to jade trees an such—they got sense enough to fend for
themselves."

I knew the tune; it went (welcome home!) like my
own, at least as I'd started to see it. I thought of myself
and my own stopped-up charts and said, "The boys don't
dig our process, girl. They dread our creative kinks."

"Not in the bed," Chloe cut in.

I laughed loud and long 'cause I had to agree. "You
know what I mean."

"Maybe so." Chloe just grinned, in the know.

"They got no use for our off&on moods, ups&downs
of direction, quick turns on a dime, any of that flipside
jive. Remember the story of Chicken Little?"

That caught her off guard; she stopped just to think.
"C.L. was all set to bake her bread, runnin around town
tryin to drum up support for her craft, askin her dear ones
to give her a hand. And they all turned real flaky, remember?" I took it all the way out, fell into fowl voice of Little
herself approaching an erstwily suitor. "*Who will help me
bake my bread?*' " I let my voice drop into bass poultry
tone. " '*Not I,*' said the little duck. *I don't give a fuck.*'"

We clowned on down, taking our leave from ill-suited
sanity til Chloe surfaced. "Umnph, umnph, umnph." She

sighed out the weary expression with thin gusts of blood-pressure wind between sighs as darkwomenfolk do. Took her a breath for the road and then: "They don't wanna see you change. . . ." Her shoulders sagged and her mouth, its boundaries turned downward again. "They want you to be the same"—she looked away—"*all* the damn time. . . ."

"Even tempered."

"Or *some*thin. Somethin I ain't got."

"Who the hell does?"

"Some a these women—"

"Some a these women got pre*tense*, baby girl. *'I'm a-fraid the mas-quer-ade . . . is o-verrrr. . . .'*" I sang the lines, knew a cue when I felt it.

Chloe didn't budge. "I don't know, girl. Maybe it's me."

"Doin what? Bein you?"

She had to give up a grin. "Not doin what they want me to."

"Such as?"

She scooted forward, edging away from my eyes. "Aw, Kamau wants me to be there for him, he sez—"

"He there for you?"

She kept her head rigid. "That's a whole nother thang." She snorted with short exhalations, short fisticuffs of stored-up spare air. "Sometimes—now maybe I'm paranoid, maybe it's *me*—"

I started to hum, ... looked at my nails til she dredged up a smile. "Sometimes, no joke though, the man seems to not only not help . . . I don't know. He seems to out-an-out undermine me."

She'd rushed out this last so I said, "Is that new?"

"On the planet, you mean? Or just in my home?" Her

grin wiggled thin in a surfeit of silence and I noted her
flip attitude, it's in line with my own seeming flipness in
time of distress— What else to do but wax flippant when
counted-on fortune shows us her slip and grins as she goes,
turning to laugh at us over one nonchalant shoulder:
"*What's wrong with you? Ain't you hip?*"

"I won't drag you with detail," Chloe said. "It all
came to a head when I told him I'd won the Warhol En-
dowment for Graphic Collage. I coudn't believe his reac-
tion." She paused for a few. "The night before Kamau was
all over me, bein so sweet, tellin me love-stuff like it was
wartime; we made love and then love—he couldn't get
enough." Her words had started to gush in a rush through
panicky rapids of tidepooling topical care. "The next day
I told him my news— I'd started to tell him last night but
I thought, Let a sleepin dog lie, cuz the award was still
formative then, it wasn't confirmed til today, an I don't talk
stuff that's in gear til it hits."

"You and me both." I considered Plexus, my wall-
flower order piano, and flashed on how my composing still
was stopped up and I'd yet to find the unstopper although
I had to and soon too, before my f'ship runs out, being the
Wurlitzer fallow-type Fellow I am, maintained on the taut-
shortening string of my grant. . . . Yet I spoke up to Chloe:
"But what happened when you ran your boon by him?
Congrats! by the way. I'm so proud of you, girl, how you
work things up for yourself." I gave her a squeeze-to-me
hug. "Heaven knows it ain't easy—"

She rolled on right by me, not taking time to note her
success or my thrill. "'Uh-huh,' Kamau said when I told
him. *Uh goddamn huh*, an that's all."

"You got ta be jivin. What'd you say?"

"He took me completely by surprise, caught me nappin." Her face had flushed rancorish red. "If you could've seen him the night just before, an like that, presto change-o, the followin day he was *cold*, honeybaby. He gave me the freeze. . . ."

"But what did he *say?*"

"Goddamnit, I told you! You with me or what?" She clenched out the words and then broke down in tears. " 'Uh-huh, uh-huh,' that Negro said, an then when I told him I was feelin let down by his lacka response, 'Oh. Congratulations,' he said."

"Just like that?"

"I wanted to say, 'You don't act like no booncoon to *me*—' But instead I just said, 'You could win too, honey; all you gotta do is keep showin your work. The powers that be put one black at a time on the throne of each art—"

"An you gotta remember you queen for a day. Just bear in mind that your throne is on wheels. Don't get to thinkin it's anchored in stone."

"When they snatch it back, all you can do is try to land on your ass. You might could break somethin you need. . . ."

Chloe had a way of saying "okay" with finality and yet with an upsurge of delay. *"Okay?"* she said slowly in this fashion then, making me grin at her effort.

"Oooooh, I still love him," she started to sing. "I oughta work your way an come up singin when times get hard."

"Yeah, well—" I broke into a chain of 'Retha's soul notes: " *'Yesterday I sang a love song . . . but to-day . . . I'm singin the . . .* [I stored up this last and then let it blast] *. . . the BLUUUES!"*

"You ain't said nothin but a word. I do dig how you work all your feelins into a song though."

"I don't know about *that*—" Plexus-thought grabbed me.

"Girl, you know it like I do: You always be workin some kinda music, even under—"

"—baldheaded circumstances." I finished it for her. "I know what you mean." I thought the rest, how Music Under just comes to me, it seems to suggest its way into the madness at hand. Some of this shit should be *scored.* Am I lyin?

"*Oooooh, I still love him, though he beats my mind; he treats me like a dog's do-do . . . doo-wah, doo-wah . . .* ain't my bag. I *hate* that shit. Still an all though, I gotta admit I ain't worked through my pull to unmuzzled men though."

I hushed my *glissando* to let her proceed.

"Hell, what he think? I been as close to there as I'm go' get; I *know* how it goes with a black man all set to let himself shine with his talent—"

"Not in this world. It ain't that kinda party.

"Say it again. I dig his changes. But what'm I spoze to do? I gotta go head an work my own show."

Chloe was getting het up, so I took it forward, felt called to cut in with an aside I thought might provide respite. "You don't want much," I said with a laugh. "All you want is the whole nine yards."

She looked at me balefully; I picked up the cue to back off. When I touched her shoulder, she started to sob and I reached out to hold her, rubbing her back as she cried freely in snatches and heaves, like I'd always wanted to yet seemingly lacked heart to let go and let flow. *Just*

work out your wrackage of anguished fem-life stopped up
for years under clamp-lids of save-face and other such self-
crush suggestion, forlornities learned to conform with, or
else.

"How you feel about funerals?" Chloe was asking.
(The bridge of *St. James Infirmary* stretched through my
mind, but I kept my dirge to myself.) "Well, you *at* one."
Chloe'd taken my mum for consent so was bent on sharing
her grief at any event, saying with pent-seeming vengeance,
"Me an Kamau is all the way through." Her eyes were
shiny with could've-been tears, so I held my center and
lent her a lyric of uplift, mind to muse-echo mind. *"It was*
just one of those things, . . . " I vibed to her, then found
myself caught in shared snare of sad pierced-through heart
times: the dart of offense seeming to issue from someplace
recessed beyond Vide, that's for sure, but beyond Karl and
certainly lately gone Nate— None of the above, the lovers
among them, had mustered the dearness to stab my heart's
core from close range, I'd made sure of that and I knew it
but didn't know *Why* yet and still; surrounding my heart
was a moat of No Admittance, no matter their lures crooned
subliminally in C-minor key.

"Honey, be good to yourself," I just told Chloe. "Keep
hangin in, because Art's one arena where a woman's equal
to a man, and black and white merge on the dance floor.
All you need's to be able to rock, rap, and *break* to the
pop aesthete beat, and a late fool can see you got good
time. So just tell Kamau where to get off. Do it like this:
Say *'Scuze me while I bugaloo!'"*

Satyrical Days:

A Feminine Phase

We'd made our way through the tunnel under the Bay and the train had roared toward the Shattuck Street Station, near where Chloe and I planned to get off. From here I could see our surrounds from afar, incomparable scene of bayside green dotted by wildcolor, wildflower growth, all of it potted by reckless-joy nature, no care for enough is enough, she plants her paradise anywhere, nevermind natives' urban hell air of not needing beauty or caring for such.

I remember last evening, after I'd played with Plexus in vain, still producing no new muse-ic or semblance of same, I'd rushed into cloud-clearing fog, jumped in the ride, and driven myself to the top of Twin Peaks where from here I'm reminded of my formal advent to this picaresque, picture-packed part of coastal country, when one of my first enigmatic introes to newfound life in Lotusland was my first sight of demarcated View Areas to which you drive from the freeway— Views had their own exits, so that as if by design and deliberate goal, in order to see your surrounds from afar, breathtaking, gladmaking chlorophyll hills everywhere a glad eye could see. Eureka! I'd found it unbounded, panoramic destiny of alluring azure on high, skies enfluffed with easy drifts of here-at-hand possible clouds and mist resisting the breeze in order to rest over ocean til nightfall with its call of the moon's timeless tide .... And steadfast redwoods, palm trees, tall hat eucalyptus—they shed sage's sight and seeds of delight at being alive and primal and fragrant with essence, *élan vital* sparkling through cortex of pith.

At the edge of the scene was hilly San Frisco, huddled and hugging her bay of sea spray, where I imagined promising sailboats to be sailing away from the urb only in order to miss her, to appreciate San Fran from afar at lovers' absent distance, where sweet pain of heart, it blooms fonder, looms past belief. It's the selfsame San Span that I saw then below, in night-glimmer light of thin fog shaking awake for the day over hills of here and there brilliant-gleam clarity, some of them seen in premature luminescence, on the cusp of crisp real and shimmer-surreal, the turnaround of time at what seems to us as dawn.

Chloe and I'd made our way via B.A.R.T. train under the Bay and exited at Shattuck Station (home of Berkeley's Humphrey Go-BART, Cal campus shuttle) near where soon we'd be swept into drama of Telegraph St. And sure as sho nuff right before us in fleetfooted matter of moments was stalwart Julia Vinograd at eternal corner of Dwight foregone Way—she wearing her ongoing beret of post-hippie days like today, said beret being funk-elegant velvet in style and fabric of bygone days of upraised idealism, open-praised ethics: the crushed rush-by sixties, still prime suspectful— Julie's blowing her atmospheric bubbles (still wields her kid's plastic bottle of Kiddie's Kick Bubbles and teeny tot's wand; "attitude correction," she calls this contribution, blowing soft tender floatinghope bubbles at hard passersby who think to themselves, *Fuck* irridescence! or something of the surly sort). Along with her luminous transient spheres Vinograd dispenses original poems in format of mini-riff chapbooks set adrift personally by poet at day-to-day work just like everyone else, except that her job's to rescue the world.

All along Telegraph there're street merchants selling wares from portable tables, one being covered in raw ruby silk and containing every possible geode under the moon: inner-earth crystals that look to have come from the nethers beneath us where tolkein folk dwell in their curly-toed knell. And another—this table's rife with rad tiny teeshirts handpainted with multihued dragons who graze in a garden of nodding balloons. Someone walks up to inspect merchandise with a toddler who wrenches away from the hand of holdback and runs toward the tees of his calling, probably thinking, *Now these, they express ME*— He's running toward fantasy shirts like a colt to his oats, bent on self-sustenance (Don't try to stop me!).

It's in light of this here on T. Street in Berkeley that I suddenly think of our shopping flipside, our pandemerican Mall with its rabid consumption of lookalike wares that include so-called service of sad beauty crank-em-out parlors— "These blondes better watch out," Chloe said once. "They startin to look like somebody's crankin em outa a bleach clone machine," and they are, someone is, in our exurban antaesthete malls of excess where everyone's blinded by mindlessly Shopping; their insight's eclipsed by u.v. Consumption.

"Do you LOVE to shop!?" read a lure-question sign that I saw in a mall once— Everyone just passed it by, except I; who but a fool reads mall fodder for thought? Now *"Final Clearance!" "Brown Flower Day!"* Well okay then, we dig *that* pabulum for dumb rumination our brain cells can gum. Put it this way: Whoever invented consume/alls should've been chewed for the good of society. I recall skidding to this conclusion when in my last final mall I spotted a sourmood kid, his tongue and attitude blued by the chemical Slurpee he guzzled; already he's hooked to that ooze, baby booze. But never fear though, there's none a that here on rife Telegraph Street—here on Tellie it's spicey and nice, without whitebread, vanilla, or suchtype bland flavor— There's only the gates we can see stretching toward us, the Sather Gate spread of U of CAL campus where we'll be accosted by politico pamphleteer troupes, then by their entrenched opponents—a preview of coming detractions that leads me to say to boon Chloe, "The moon must be in fooldom today."

We'd stopped off in Moe's and then Cody's to dig on the latest largess of lit, namely new/found/land, nouveau-type, forward ho! fiction. So it's thus that we'd left with near nothing at all but for a back issue of sound *Solid Ground* that I'd bagged and Alexis DeVeaux's *Don't Explain* (put out years ago by a petrified press) that Chloe'd snagged, then we'd gone to an eat place named Counter Culture and seated ourselves at a counter with tall stools for two to the left of the door. I took a gander at Chloe in her bright fuchsia paint-dotted smock to which she'd affixed

a ridged amber pin of lucite or alkyd—I couldn't tell; it
seemed to be from the forties. *We must make for a hell of
a match*: the thought came and went, off the wall. . . . I
was sporting my crimson sundress with matching *huraches*,
my groundswell of hair being done up in shoulder-length
braids, what could be 3003 of these brushing my back and
one side of my face with their fuzz, brushing pests of a
persistent species, seeming to buzz.

I'd told Chloe, yet weirdly had yet to show and tell
me the real story of my men and myself, how I hid in their
fleshly connection in order to *ground* and how I was
wrenched to the past for fulfillment it seemed, then I
thought *No, I'd best keep my glueball of thought to myself,
just suggest that I've got my own share of woes: I've got
blues too.*

"Wait," Chloe was saying. "Let me catch up. You
gotta allow for me; I'm sorta slow."

"A deliberative thinker."

"No. *Slow.* An honey, you make me feel slower."

I looked away, already intuiting what she had to say.

"No bout adoubt it, I can see you wrapped up in some
sorta head thang. What the hell is it though?"

"Tell me and we'll both know."

With pale xanthic fingers she covered my hand still
holding its impotent fork. "Whatever your trip is, it don't
seem to have done you much damage." The tone she was
using had a catch to it, a strange sort of silly singsong
that seemed to sing its own strain in subkey beneath the
topside of her words, a *there there now* mocking refrain.
"I hope you don't mind," she said careful-weirdly. "All
I'm try—"

I cut her off. "What you're trying to do is the usual, what I'd expect. Spare me your overdue care."

She snatched back her hand, rose to my flare. "You awfulass touchy for someone who lives in a dream. I didn't mean that," she said on the heels of her spite, before it had scurried from view. She was looking into my eyes for permission to free her from guilt—*Are we all right?*

Her scare didn't faze me; I was caught in amazed accusation that right then had wrestled its way to topside astride me. I was caught in a dream and I didn't know why I was haunted, just knew I was caught in snafu of no composition, no music of mine, yet some sort of detox solution seemed at the verge of my dam, trying like hell to work its way through.

Somewhere in space I heard Hamiett Bluiett blowing from down in a well up and out through the bell of his baritone sax; Willie Colon just had joined in his role in rerun of a fabulous set I'd dug in the Big Apple Core before making tracks for the West— In my mind's ear Hamiett continues to blow, now playing *"Straight From The Heart,"* a knockmedead jam that he works upward and over from bends of his knees so mighty sax elbow, it rests there in inches of space, suspended, held barely in place by hard-working neckstrap above as self-snatching baritone notes herald their way through horn's supersize spout rendered from magical brass stoked and attended by Thoth-spirit elves. I remember how one hapless night in the Village, there in the knell, I'd bumbled into the green of Sweet Basil's to find by the way of my ears that Lo! there appearing as star in the East was mystical Hamiett Bluiett, magi returned from near-recent tour with his whole constellation,

World Sax. And it came to pass that with no ado I found myself Chosen thus treated to *sirius* sound of World Sax Quartet: waypaving Dave Murray and Oliver Lake at their tenors—Lake with native indigenous nose and always urb-Indian hat o'er his dreads—while less than a note's throw behind them looms tall-*soma* Julius Hemphill sounding hallowed alto as Atlas of W.S.Q.

"Kat, you here or not?" Chloe levels at me with sharp rustic bark in her voice. "Thought we was togethuh, kid-sister. You make me feel like I'm here all alone."

"I thought you knew, I'm here on my own and you're on yours too—"

"Meanin what?"

"You ain't ready for this."

"I'm ready for you."

I'd play her off so I thought, and already was looking away when she went on to say her particular *say*.

"Kat, you real heavy into my bizness to be so light on sharin your own. I feel just like I don't know you. . . ."

Her rancor spewed out in the form of sarc banter, but I turned her down *sotto voce* in mind and proceeded to think what I knew: I was feeling low rez so I needed to walk and I needed to talk to myself; I was long overdue. *I need a reality check* was the lone solo note that came through, so when Chloe tapped my hand and showed me her smile of all's almost well saying, "Come on, difficult one, we'll grab us some shortbread from Just Desserts, then move on to Sacred Grounds for our coffee,"

"No, I gotta get on," I said to her swiftly, and cinch-brushed a kiss on her cheek. "Catch you on the upswing."

"I'm sorry we hassled."

"Girlfriend, please. No regrets."

> *. . . no mat-tuh what you say or do,*
> *I'lllll say good-bye*
> *with no regrets. . . .*

Ladyday's voice jagged in a jig through my heart with Benny Carter honkytonk tumbling on clarinet behind her as I hurried up Dwight Way to Shattuck, haunted by audio visions of times gone before. Yet I thought then, *these riddling dreams, maybe they'll fuse a new* alla breve *type bridge to my muse.* I'd yet to figure my onstreaming fantasies featuring sisterly Kitty and Lena and son, the man called Chicago . . . yet the past was the place to go when I was mad, sad, or too glad to stand it; past eras were full of more life than the *now* where I sustain my self-inflicted identity— That's how I'd describe the nature of me: I'm a woman in search of my own need to *be.*

Look at my hook-ups with Karl, Vide, and Nate (make that Nate, Karl, and Forgotten; there's no need for Vide)— I can't help but notice how much of my current is twined in sad skein of twist-tangled game after game. I've heard from Nate yet again by way of his most recent phonecall left in remote on my diligent tape, Nate the great bizBUP of strategic reports called to me via hasty long-d. In gen, he's okay and still on the case among workerbee whites and their engineered blacks who cut him with exacto-edge scorn for his determined recruitment of unspoken blacks held at safe distance bay. Thus and no wonder Nate's struggling solo with more than one type of on-the-job prob. Harddriven Nate—undefeated fave of my formative future,

best runninbuddy to be who I've yet to see lately in this
sidelong dance of frenzied time. He's nine-to-fived in appearance as he fades into memoried focus. . . . I see him
now as he was then when we last encountered and hugged
our *goodbye*, no, our *til we hook later.* . . .

I gave him my doe eyes til he laughed and broke free.

"You know what? The whole world's vanilla and chocolate," he told me. "Now what sort of flavor are you?" He
nuzzled the side of my neck on a sudden. "Ummmm—I
taste outerspace. But I won't let it faze me. I dig the taste
of wild game." He hugged me to the tweed of himself, so
that I was caught in his warmth and tobacco/y smell, fallible
fumes of the flesh. "Did you miss me?" He laughs at
himself.

"Of course I missed you, what do you think? You're
the man of my dreams and you left me bereft—"

"Uh-oh, now, don't overdo."

"Where were you anyway?" (Mundanity grabs me; it
pulls me through.)

"At our Affirmative Traction convention."

"There're enough of you for a convention?" I bumbled,
then stood mouth agape, a bumblestum still.

"We're an endangered species, of course. In these
post-Raygun years we've been shelved and backburnered
galore. We met in New York."

"In the Big Apple Core."

"Where there are parts you can barely digest. The
rest isn't meant for human consumption."

I dinkensed away to the first friendly tangent. "No
wonder you're looking so fit. Where'd you get this?" (his
dap-collared shirt of sheer cotton lawn)

"At the Goodwill."

"Come on now, Nate, don't try to jive me."

"See?" he says as if to himself. "You try to give em the truth and they give it right back. What's wrong with Goodwill?"

"Not a thing, but you wouldn't know, knowin you. Nigguh, you stay two jumps aheada *G.Q.*"

Without rue he dropped back into badblack verknack. "See how they 'mouth you? Why you don't cut me no slack?" Then to my grin, after which he was gone, "You'll see me soon. I'll be back."

It's in slack frame of mind that I think next of Karl as I enter the subway and wait to board B.A.R.T. I imagine I see him debarked from a train down the track, then look back again just to assure me of my knack for observing hensteeth-type spectacles seldom seen or cared for by naked normal eyes, and I see him, I do, there goes Karl accompanied by a lithe young feminine thing full of flourishing gestures and cameo poses, a *poseur au fond, dernier cri,* news to me; she must be or could be an actress Karl's wearing as 3-D costume. "Karl!" I call once in authoritarian register—at least I hope that it's so, and it is; a thousand heads turn, among them is Karl's, said head frowns and then grins when he sees me, now frowns again as he turns in brief speech to nube-female lead and then urges her toward me. In still-distant greeting, Karl's waving what looks like a goatherder's gnarled *feta* stave, "Kat . . . *love,*" he intones as that image fades and another vision rolls by:

Along comes a guy who draws my eye by the way that he carries himself in erect self-possession or semblance of such—from far away I make him out as he drops what looks to be a ticket, a piece of paper, tiny, which flutters from his grasp but only for an instant, til he reaches out to catch it with a snap before it reaches even knee level— That gesture is what grabs me, that catlike snatch of what's one's own from jaws of would-be downward destiny, nevermind surrounding apathy and with a smile that— I see him throw his head back in playful self-approval, his thumbs are tucked in taut suspenders of his ego, no doubt— Ego yields resiliency which manifests as head held high above quick-tempoed bouncing stride. Look at him walk, sure-footed, straight-ahead, unafraid of flex—adjustment *is his middle name, adaptability his baby.*

He strides toward my eyes opened wide/steps to me and I see that it's Karl, unrecognizable except for his flair, newly coiffed (his hair's cut into a front, all else is bare but triangular mohawk of tall heady kinks), haute coutured *in his baggy now suit of worsted dark tweed with thin* See me? *type stripe running through). A small smile creases his face for an instant then fades right away, Spoof! as quick as it's been.* . . . *He tugs gently at one side of jacket so that lingering wrinkles subside if they're there.*

Then look at Karl as he looks at himself, flicks fleck of lint from his image, Karl-Actor lends smile that's just so, just a tease with lips closed—his profile looks better that way due to barely stick-outy teeth he keeps tucked; also pressure of pressed lips, it activates on-and-off clefts. His posture's firm-footed, braced for appraisal then sale. Karl with his dusk-tinted skin of secret intent, he's looking at me . . . *now cocking handsome-boned head to the side, acting as if we're alone; he scarcely notices others it seems, looks at me straight on, nonstop, with eyes unblinked to mesmerize.*

"What is it you get out of sex?" Karl asked me once, not long heretofore.

"What I put into it." What could I say? That *sex is my lure, it acts as my moor to the world of response.* . . . I was in no mood for Karl's straightforward jabs; frankness has to be welcome or toleration prone. Instead, the face of my lying there beside Karl moved me to warmed-over aftermaths of less taxing times and places and sexual spaces that left no room for regret, or for fretting through future floes alone, disarmed by the loss of myself to a calling I couldn't pin down even yet. Something wrenched me, it tried to redeem me, to free me from frame-up. Look at my crime: I've tried to kill time. . . .

The light of Karl's smile seems to glare and grow brighter. "What is it you get out of me?"

"Now Karl dear, you know." (I've planned to decline his show of great show.)

"I know what you give me to know, which is little or nothing of you. You're so close to the chest about you. Where are you? Who are you? I never can find you; I still don't know you that well—"

"What the hell does that mean?"

He leans toward me and looks into my eyes. I bristle for a moment, caught in his net. "It means," he says clearly, "words, words, and more misunderstood words, all of them unneces—"

I stop his mouth with my kiss, a forethought move that leads me to close my tired eyes to unbearable dullness without, so that I'm lost in the brilliance of self, suffused as it is by unwanted strange vision, *déjà vu* memory, one of the few that refuses to melt.

"You want romance? Baby, I'll give you romance!"

I was sitting in the bathroom full of sun and shadows, my favorite room in the flat due to its plants and bamboo beneath brazen skylight, just right moist warmth of lush growth and brown bodies in bloom. . . .

Karl had coaxed me to the toilet seat where I've leaned back into welcoming cloth-padded porcelain, a brace for my back as Karl blots bathwater from my skin's surface with a rough-tufted terrycloth towel which he wads and discards in order to drink dew directly from tropical flesh aflush with flash heat. The extravagant rapture of full lushgrown lips— Karl's afric-legacy lips kneading round boundaries of circular areas here at my knees, and now there, at antiphonal nipples. The touch of his tongue— He licks down to indented spiral of navel, now leads tonguetip's greed to the heart of curlybushed guardian hair and whispers then, "Ummm, you taste tangy, like lemon gelato." He licks sticky liquid from my eager-throb clit, then leans back for an instant in which I manage to taste his tumescence; I've placed the palm of my hand on his belly's decline into pubis so I can see and dig drama: the rise of his root. Strength caught in motion's what I yearn to feel and so steel myself to resist before— "Ahhh. Wait/don't/Karl/stop—" I steel to resist his further fond sucks, the lick-flick of probing tonguetip so I'm able to grip the shaft of his maleness and thrill for a moment at sinew's intensity-throb through dense muscle. It's precisely this pulse that I need to squeeze with my walls of frank feminine welcome, so it must be, it is urgent business, transfusion two-sided that activates reflex to guide him inside me.

Karl fronts before me.
"You're a sweet Kitty Kat."

"I don't know about that." I could feel Kitty, she welled up inside me. *They think I'm sweet. Must be cuz a my lips an round eyes. Maybe if I slit my eyes so, an tuck in my lips like this, it'd give me more of an edge.*

What I tell Karl:

"I think of myself as a lemon drop—sugary on the outside, and tangy as fuck after that."

It was colder than a warlock's dick, the coldest day of the year, the fifth day of May in Frisco's own recalcitrant way; I had the heat in my flat turned up to max when the furnace broke down on a sudden, lickety split. I had a fit, knowing full well the snafu was due to my resident gnome, gnomely Maldorer my maintenance demon, devil's main imp that he was. What next? I said to myself bogged in fog of the nabe I call home on my hill near the ocean's first roll of iced seafull air. When parking sad Sexus, my *no ops* jalopy (and finally home to my heat! so I thought), I'd made out two Frisco natives in down jax and scullcaps, hunched as they were in bold scurry to shelter, then I'd made way past tourists in shorts damnear shivered to stone, all alone in their plight of expecting San Fran to be like L.A., which S.F.'s not in any farfetched sort of way, let alone in her temp; she works her own clime on her own type of time. Look at these tourists! I'd said to myself— seeing them lifted my spirits. As I headed inside to my overdue warmth I'd sneered a weird grin of pleasure-packed glee, pitifully purposeful, smug, sad on me. . . .

There was no time to waste, Karl was en route for our prearranged date, he'd be here in a few, so my pre-schemed Plan A was to fix up the place, while overt Plan B was to leave home melee as it festered and just fix up me. *"Nail Him . . . TONIGHT!"* read a billboard just moments ago

that I'd noted although I know I'm uncosmetic and hope-
lessly so—*"NAIL HIM TONIGHT! (With Nails That Are
Longer And Stronger Than Your Own, Yet Look So Natural
He'll Never Know They're Not! Nails You Can Buy Today
And Wear Tonight—Sculptured GEL NAILS & NAIL GEL,
both by Jonêl.)"*

That's the ticket, I thought for a twist of cyclical time,
picturing me with plexiplast fingertips poised at poor
Plexus. Just focus on such stuff as nails of your fingers,
nevermind wrangles of head like making your music and
decoding dreams of past history times you keep seeming
to find yourself in. Soon I'd be prepping for Karl for a
passel of reasons, foremost among them the need to not be
alone on my chimeric own— It's like Lena said once, in
one of her mindstage appearances to me: "If we were meant
to be alone, we wouldn't be born under social circumstances, among our fellow fools." Besides which, in being with
Karl I'd be showing my bigness of spirit—so went the strat;
I'd let him know no hard feelings had tartared and calcified
from our set-to when we'd last rendevoused.

But already the doorbell was ringing with scarcely a
chord of transition, and Karl'd made his comeback, ta-
bleauxed for a time in protective turtleneck sweater and
his stark casual jeans of today, strangely ordinary looking
except for a chest-resting pendant featuring joined visage
of trag/com/edy—"two faces of the same reality," Karl told
inquisitive me.

"Good God, where's your heat?" he took leave to ask.

"Well—" I began.

"Lunch? You want lunch?" he said, satisfied. "I'll
cook you lunch! We'll have what your sweet heart desires."
He strode to the kitchenette zone and burrowed like Browso

the Beaver all through the fridge while I moved to the couch and sat within view. Karl winked at me smileless. "Kat, I never know what you're going to do."

Let me know when you manage, I thought, *and then share it with me.*

"No problem of course," he said in a rush. "I dig spontaneity, see."

The notion of pre-set direction was leagues from my mind; not from his though, which seemed to suggest a closet conformity to old shoe shod tried and trueblue. What prompted his pretext or new-contoured ruse? Would it come from a free fellow artiste in that straightup cliché type of way? "He protesteth too much," Shakespeare, my main bard, had jumped bad to say.

Karl was bustling with gusto; he looked like the Frugal Gourmet sauced and then peppered to potent spiced vim. "Once you asked me," he said, "if I like to act."

(I'm keeping impassive as actively possible.)

"That teed me off," he went on. "I never ask if I like it or not; I *have* to act, or I'll develop toxemia from all the toxins boxed up inside me. What about you? Do you like to compose?"

I knew what he felt and yet couldn't tell him. I figured he'd use it against me. (Or so I said: I proffered this view to the keeper of hype in my head.)

Karl turned to face me. " *'I'll not be found wandering the streets, chasing the ghost of what I should have been.'* Who said that?"

"Paul Robeson."

Karl gave me a seeming-insidious wink. "You've felt that way yourself, right?"

"Wrong," I said. "Next?"

He turned his back to me— I made out his grin when he accidentally turned profile and cheesed to the side.

"I figured it out." I said with a smile.

"What's that?" He stopped rustling and stiff-jawed a yawn.

"Where you're coming from." (He raises brows, tired, but I don't let it raze me; I just hunker forward, into his wind.) "You don't know *me* because you're so into you."

"Kat, Kat, Kat— What *is* it you want?" His face flickers on for a moment. He's throwing diced chicken into an overhot wok . . . stands back to dig with approval . . . searches for mega-diced celery and throws that in too with no further ado. "Say what you may," he tosses at me. "At least I have nerve enough to flesh out my dream."

I'm taking time to bounce back when he turns for a moment to face me. "Kat, what's the problem?" He braces.

"Do you even want to know me?"

He turns the heat up for a wooden-mimed moment in time. "Ask me that later, when I can show you. You know what though? You've got a real obtuse point of view."

I refurled my ego and tucked it safely inside me, far away from possible panic to be. I'd been brooding about pressure against my own pith, why I push over so freely as thin spindly sapling to winds of strong ire, and to internal gusts of strong reverie. But then I see that Karl's staring at me for Coptic eternity til billows of blackness appear in the sight, smell, and form of combustablaze smoke with a glare in its trail that dully I realize must be a fire— Then comes a series of unexplained scenes that rage for attention as unseemly dream:

I see people running, folks in the forties, among them a tall-hatted man who turns just to show me he's 'Go. . . .

Then enter nightriders marauding with brickbats enblackened by blood of the colored.... A-reeee! sounds a firewagon's dopplering siren, a firewagon racing right up to a woman who's worn and still wearing mourned ashes of life: a woman I see who is me.

But Karl's crashing my musement with concrete concern. "Goddamnit, you idiot, *help* me!"

"Oh," I say stupidly, still coming to and mad 'cause caught napping while—I real/eyes now—Karl's flash-dousing flames wherever he can. So what do I do? I rush to the hall for my ace fire extinguisher, only to feel some sort of omen as soon as I've grabbed it. . . .

"Let's see." I stand reading. "*'HOLD UPRIGHT. PULL RING PIN.'*" (What's a 'ring pin'? Like we've all got one we use every day, soon's we pee maybe, or've just had done with brushing our teeth—but fuck it, read on and be glad for this boon you hold here in your hands, just read on and the instrux'll come clear.) "*'PULL RING PIN. Stand 8 to 12 Feet From Fire. Press Lever.'*" (What lever? *Where?*) "*'Direct Discharge At Base of Flame With Side To Side Motion. Then . . .'*"

Karl snatched the canister from me—"Give *me* the damn thing. I'll *work* it, not read it"—which he proceeded or so thought to do and would've done too, but for the fact that Maldorer'd come first and denatured the thing, so when Karl pulled the release ring and force-pressed the nozzle, instead of a groundswell of on-the-spot foam, a thin milky stream of liquid leaked out, oozing in late sorry drips onto Karl's Bally shoes.

"I should've known," I heard him mutter as both of us snatched for whatever we could—I'm dousing the black crackling wok of our would-be cuisine with precious

garbanzo-bean flour; Karl's smashing everything glass in
his wake as he crashes about with a handful of towels. I'd
just seen the flash of his eyes through receding flames when
he turned to roil rancor at me.

"If you hadn't been so intent on sitting on your ass
til the fucking last minute—"

I was browned off, fired by my ire. "I thought you
had everything under control."

He took a look at the room in a wreck and his features
softened into a smile. "Just to be sure," he stagewhispered
as if to himself as he quick-filled a skillet with water and
then dumped it nimbly all over me there in the spot where
I stood. "Now will you wake the hell up?" he cheshired to
me.

That put the knaps on the afro. "Man, have you lost
your last screw?" I out and out shouted. "I thought you
could *hang* if something came up, like I do."

Karl flexed to the challenge, using his wordways as
weapons I tried to combat though I could hear my half of
our sound as wounded *staccato* subdued in battle by hands-
down *longato*. We were badmouthing back like two low-
minded loons— I had to stop us before who knew what,
so I snatched myself up by the scruff of my rage and said,
"Karl?" (to which he skids: "Huh?") *"Damn if I know where
this madness came from. Let's just call this one square and
all's fair!"*

To the Edge

of the Rainbow:

A Song Named

"Chicago"

Without impulse of Karl and the others I'm sucked toward the vortex of meaning for me, away from mucous of upcoming life with its probable strife, into overlife rapids that wash away my life of today and rush me toward whirlpooling dream in high gear.

MMM, come to me/be my succor or suck-juicy remedy/ sure cure for root rot/these down-to-earth dues with their consequent blues!

Why'd I waste time with Karl? Inside I still chafed and knew I'd continue til I knew the answer or saw it at least: I'd use this man as he'd use me, as a thing to stave off the worst thug of all, the feminized mugger called destiny. Karl's body for me was my groundforce, connection to earth and therefore rebirth into now, away from the past that arced up as highcrested waves to claim me. I had to capture myself in the current, so searched for male grail in order to do it, to *focus*/get to it, and away from recall, hey, of yestersad/day.

AND OOH, BAYBEE BAYBAY . . . HE KNOWS *JUST WHAT TO DO. . . .* 'Go's stepped up to the beckoning bandstand, leans now into liquid slow hornnotes of relentless refrain/dimensionalized pain: wails muted by spherical spinout through low throaty sax, the man's magic *ax*—it's his mode of modality; he's just made it ours, that raspy low whispering voice of innermost longing and sharp inner tucked-away strife under wraps until now— 'Go makes his horn lose its hornhood, sound like the whispering imp in your mind who's watched you and knows you so now blows your story in primeval prose disguised as a series of musical letters called *notes* that spell out your life in rash statements of chords— Sweet release! The music whines for you/croons to you with ease/please! just don't stop/op scrop *do* she-bop/It hails you and soothes you/then flails you/but SCOOP! Diddley op/it bounces you over your home in earth-hell/lifts you two/make it three broad crooked airtides to the side/of mainstream straight-n-narrow/to where sound becomes sight/and the gash-rent globe seems whole again/to long-range ears/and outlandish eyes—

No doubt about it, just hear that horn! 'Go's a wraith who's appointed to relay the gospel, and never you fear, the man stays on his *j*— See? What did I say? No sooner than his saga's received, already it's transmitted back drenched in white light of transcendent *in-sight.* I love Chicago like this, as one with music made mine for a time, the man and his muse on the One.

'Go strides toward me after his solo but stops on the path—he's caught in a thicket of fans. From my outlook here in mid-gloom of the music hall room, I see

his profile not flaccid yet loose, tall and resilient, leaned
forward a moment, extending himself to well-wishers in
his own open style. *Nothin to it but to do it. . . .* I'm a
fool for this cat Chicago, my nose stays wide open, don't
tell me, I know. And now, right this moment, he looks
up like I've called him, his jaw-dimple flashes my way
and then winks. I softside smile back and can't help it,
I tap my left wrist as if it's a watch, at which 'Go nods
and grins further, speed-greets devotees in uptempo time,
reaches to touch one chick's would-be-blessed shoulder,
doling her rash reassurance— Then here he comes, lank-
striding up to my table, leaning to kiss me: *"How did
we do? We get to you?"* Muteness removes me, I can't
bear to speak—

   'Go's nodding toward his quartet still on the stand:
They're blowing off steam of an outswinging dream, down-
under dynamics now that 'Go's gone—Cleanhead's on
trumpet, blazing through waves of postwar weary fog; Mingus mans bass, running through undergirth changes;
Maxroach tames traps, melody mad as a musicman's
high—he'll wrest a tune from these rhythm snares yet,
brushes highhat cymbalic pies in orderly counterpoint and
oomp! sprickledy *splish:* those cymbals, they dish up—
Work it on through!—new-subdued dissonance, thunder-
clap days full of bolts from the blue. . . .

   We soak it all up, don't bother to talk til 'Go takes
the stand again once and for all at the end of the spree,
then he splits for his usual *few* of stretched time in which
I'm pricked with worry, yet manage to manage myself afterall: So 'Go's had him some *boo. Well, he works real hard
too.*

   "We'll all fall by Chollie's. How's that?" 'Go puts his

arm around me, hugs me to the scent of his energy. I'm digging the spice of his sweat, soaking that synergy, just can't help it, I'm all the way gone from the set.

"Tell you what," 'Go says to me across the table of our booth at Chollie's—he's holding a mug of steaming coffee in one square-knuckled hand, itself the color of coffee, high-strung dream beans and cream—"I'm too far gone to turn back now. On the level. If I can't do this thing" (his art/to follow his muse in a muse-echo way), "I can't do nothin at all." He takes a long draught from his mug.

"You sayin there's nothin else you'd make yourself do? Suppose—now don't get me wrong—but suppose somethin happened so you couldn't play, at least for a time." I cut myself off to sip me some tea; I was treadin thin surface, so knew to tiptoe on through. "You got a second-string thing you could work, just somethin to fall back on, now don't you? If push comes to shove—" I made it my business to look past his questioning eyes.

"What is it you tryin to say?" He sliced through my ruse.

I fumbled for time til "I got you," he smiled like new sunlight, a strong flash of bright, those gaphappy pearl whites of his. . . .

I was grinning in spite of myself. "No joke now, 'Go."

He smiled again, this time at my grin. In thin self-defense I looked off and went on. "I can't picture you, not all the way down, not with nothin to brace you." I'd fessed up: I was worried again, again about nothin, to 'Go's point of view. Accordin to him, I lived in a lather of *What if?*

disaster, high-foam Fels Naptha of what'll never happen any damn way. Hell, didn't I know colored folks live on the fly, from day to quick day? "Just dig our talk and our music if you need a clue. . . ."

"You know somethin I don't?" 'Go was sayin.

"Come again?"

"What's wrong with what I'm doin right now? Plenty folks I know dig it." He reached forward to play with my fingers, to declaw words gone before. "Honey, you forward-thinkin—"

"I hope the hell so."

"Don't you see though? That puts you in a shaky position—"

"Says who? Ask me for a change and I'll tell you: I feel just fine bein *out*." He stopped to chuckle.

"For cryin out loud, 'Go, you know how long it takes crits an wax macks to catch up with your music—"

"Only the new stuff—"

"But that's what you doin now, mostly new stuff—"

"That's the idea." He looked pleased.

"Suppose they leave you in the lurch? 'Fans is fickle as hell,' you said it yourself. An the wax biz machine, the gangs at the top . . ."

"Kit, Sweetness, I'm doin what I got to do. That's all there is to it."

"You think I don't know it? But that's just what'll leave you out in the cold—"

"Kit, listen at me."

"Why? Mister Man, you got somethin to say?"

He flipped me a grin. "Was the sun out today? This here's what I'm here for: to play now-sound regardless. I got a song in me that's gotta come out—a wild, loud, strong song of Outside I'm swagger; inside I'm . . . soft. What choice have I got but to pull out the stops?" He saw me look away but went on to say, "As for folks who don't dig what I'm puttin down, they'll catch my drift—"

"When?"

"In their own time." He tapped the table in uneven beat. "Dig," he put this to me on q.t. "when you do somethin new, you're nowhere already. That's the game's name." He leaned his frame forward and turned my face toward him with one stretched-out hand. "Don't you see, tenor lady? I can't let that stop me."

"Who said it should?" I took the occasion to quick-switch my pitch.

I couldn't shake him; he stayed right with me. "I gotta go for what I know. Damn all the rest. LOOK OUT, I'M COMIN THROUGH!" He gave up some rue in his smile focused down at the table's blank shine.

I don't know what it is, this gloom that settles around me at times/seems to ooze all into me like blues on the downbeat 'thout hope of relief. Some sorta sad an low scene comes to mind in a funeral pall. 'Nough a that though, me an 'Go, we're really much alive an we're kickin, though sometimes not high. . . .

We were making our way through trees and benches abandoned at the turnaround of night into day, apt scene for Chicago's famed "I Didn't Know What Time It Was," his nocturne of internal daybreak, eternally modified dream caught in liquefied coming to be, mad melody made of fast freedom-filled notes, *urgency* being the name of this game we run scared in—'Go's song's on the wing as sun touches land.

He pulls me to him with one easy arm. "This is my prime time of day," he confesses, lops me his smile.

"Sunset, and sunrise too 're both mine. I dig when the world disappears but for me on the sly, doin my honor to sunrise."

"That's my style too. Your main man gets high offa sunrise—"

"And in it too." I catch my own *vex*, its insistent edge, 'cause I'm thinkin of 'Go an his crack of dawn "call" as I call it, his nudge to more dope when it's bout that *time*, his cue to lost hope. It was my first clue, one I'd insisted on missing at first: the way he tore outa the crib each day at dawn, or en route from the club made his regular run. I'd only thought, before I got wise, Well the man needs to spend time alone; he's an artist, a great one, a genius, no jive—

'Go smiles his soft pastel grin, looking at sky with a boy's innocent joy. Look at that profile, the crags of his face— I'm a fool for strong bone structure; his and my own.

"Why's the world like it is, when all we need's this." He gestures at air that we're able to see now as fine dust's swirled by currents of atmosphere caught in offbeat glare. "Kitty." He stops and turns me toward him with that mild-disturbed look that I dig; it means I distract him, and *Good!* my heart says.

"What makes you put up with me?" He easeworks the query toward me, then doesn't wait for my feedback— he reaches to squeeze me, looks in my eyes, sees my worry and pain, lowers his head for a moment, looks at me squarely and says, "Kitty, I'll kick it. You'll see."

Nothing to Lose:

My Blues-Echo Muse

I was seated at Plexus when the shadow of Lena came in.

"Where can I set my valise?" she asked me; then to my dumbfounded numbness, "I'll put it right here," she said, looking at me first, then at the room with its paintings and such, images all of places and passages elsewhere. She paused at the side of my favorite featuring steps that lead to a lair just above, yet only partially visible.

"You need a lead and I'm here to provide it," she said simply, coming to sit down beside me there on my bench of decision where I sat taking note of no notes forthcoming from me. She sat not beside me but in me and of me; her form seemed to mesh with my own. Her warmth merged with mine and the shine of her presence shimmered within me so that I felt more than heard each of her words.

"You know why you've brought me," she said. "I'm

here to help you let loose that hide-and-seek sound that you're struggling to find."

I let a sonng. . . . I could make out dim lyrics light-hearted-lilting through hesitant measure. "To help me find my lost music?" I lurched in and said.

"I'm here to help you find your lost *you.*"

I warmed to the smile in her serious style, thinking to sorry sad disengaged self, I don't care who you are or where you came from, if you've got my Rx in the bag you've brought with you, you're welcome to work up my pitiful show. Whatever you've got, it's a Go!

She laughed when she heard me, though I'd yet to mouth any of this; my thoughts were unformed embryo words.

"I told you before," she said then to my confusion. When? Where had she given her counsel "before"? "Let yourself go," she continued. "In order to grow, girl, you've got to move backward through time as you know it. *Feel* what I tell you. What you need is a sense of yourself with the firm understanding that talent's the spring bud of ancestral roots. Think on it. You know it already as I do." Her presence expanded, a grandswell of song. "Don't you remember the last time we met and hitched souls? I told you before, when you were only a pitiful hatcheck girl hanging on to the glow of my boy, Chicago. Don't you recall how your music was coming to surface to save you? It was before the fire that you knew. . . ."

Jagged edges of fate came together in crags and on-wending memory whirlwinded in.

"Don't try to run me, Kitty—I'll say it again and that's it. I never blow the same riff twice. You know how I can't stand an echo."

You livin your life in the hard heart of one. It's squeez-in the juice outa you *an* your music— *I'd said it inside, with not enough pride to push me to outspoken spunk.*

Just leave me alone in my spree to destroy me— *Chicago was bound an bent to mess himself up an intent on pullin it off all alone. It got to me like nothin I knew of in life—my own griefs an gripes took a sad second to each cliffedge ramble of 'Go's. Why'd he want to stay caught in this bramble? He'd get an edge to his voice an a set to his chin an proceed to eat himself up like it was his callin. Why'd he stay tangled in bunk?*

"Well this just beats everything. Get a loada this." 'Go turned to me. "The cat musta milked this shit down, with what, I don't know. He'd started to pace, shaking his head. "I'll just be a—"

I'd had it. "You'll just be a junkie, is what you'll just be!"

"Come on, have a heart."

"And no head. Is that the idea?"

"What're you barking about?"

"Why don't you just call it quits."

He stopped in his tracks. "You're a smart cookie. You've got somethin there." *He made like a dummy, riddled an dunced by what thought could do. I talked to myself til I knew the score: He don't mean that. He's just nervetight an sore.*

"Right this moment," *I told him.* "I'll be right here to give you a hand."

"Or a foot." *He stopped to grin an then said,* "With the Roseland gig comin up? You ain't real."

"What's it to you? Just one gig—" *(But it's BIG. . . .)*

"*Now what do you think?*"

"*You said it yourself. You gotta quit sometime.*"

"*Just not right now.*"

"*Why not now? It runs a hard second to Never.*"

"*You oughta know better by now. You've stuck with me long enough to get wise.*"

"*Haven't I though. I've started to feel the battle fatigue—*" *The notion of war makes me see death, an she's draggin her sickle behind her. Got a grin on her skeleton mug fixed at me an I see* oh no! *one shinin hell light down at 'Go too. Let me change that thought good an quick. If it comes to death duty, we'll do it and just could be already ready cause I hear that dirge knell at times, always did hear it, an no doubt about it, 'Go's wise to it too.*

"*Baby, just let me hold twenty. You know I gotta get straight, an this stuff here's no damn good.*"

"*Brother oh brother. I don't know about you, but to me that looks like your cue.*"

'Go takes some steps, looks weirdly aside, then straight at me. "*You know what?*"

"*Not a thing. You tell me.*"

He wrenches his body to face me then, all of a sudden. "*This beats a dead dog to death. What do I look like to you? A native in need of his own pocket missionary? Answer me this: Is you or aincha? You in my corner or not?*" *He reaches to touch me an grips me instead. My nerves play their tune on frayed endings. . . . I feel myself squirm from his grasp an turn on a tendril to head for the door.*

"*You leave when I'm down, you leave me for good!*"

"*Since when?*" *I countered, on my way out.* "*I've put in my time!*"

"*Sweet enough duty, it looks like to me.*" He offers his slendertime grin. "*You think I don't do my share? I stay at the post a lot longer than you.*"

"*So you can feed that white mare you keep saddled. What is it, my fault you feel her hot breath on your neck? That's the edge of her teeth you feel now in your dope-sorry head—*"

"*Just get the motherfuck* out *then. Go on an split. Make it quick.*" He made a move toward me.

I know my exits. "*Fly low, Chicago, I'm* gone." I started to step up my pace to leave 'Go an then suddenly on the outside all I could see was folks runnin around me, an Chicago, he's eased out beside me to jitterhand guide me through the throng in which I make out the flash of red coat, velvet, no suede. . . . the face of a girl in her twenties, a woman in furs . . . a youngster, young boy whose face fills with dismay . . . a coal cart, an icebox, a fly Duesenberg an a roadster with arch runnin boards— A swell snatches a phonograph box from a window new-broken by a guy still holdin his show-n-tell bat. . . . Next to that is a heavyset madam who snatches the hand of her goggle-eyed toddler urging him, "*Pick up your feet!*" so that they can make haste with the hot goods she's got. Flames sprout all over, down at the horse trough for mounted hawkshaws an in brash flarin clusters that pockmark the hellblazin street. Everyone with God's sense was quick on the lam, bigots with branches of trees, an the colored on foot with their goods or just bricksticks runnin from micks with hardheart revolvers an billies— Whomp went a nightstick upside a cat's startled head, an 'Go tells me, "*We gotta break faster!*" so that we hightail out fleet feet past beefy-faced cops on the sly an never give truck to the grim scene beside us the color of *blood an scream-sound of release when a sufferin sinner meets heaven here in the streets of his heretofore hell named K.C. A "riot," they'd call it, or come to— I heard the words once before from my mama's told tales of War One: how colored GI's came back to the same old attack of slums an glum future called blest if free from lynch mobs even there in the city, East Saint Louie, she said. But the—* "Help! Mama! Mama!" *I hear a girl cry, then I look an I see she's near the same age as me, grabbin what's left of her gown down around her—an up near the corner—don't look; oh my Lord but I do—up near the street's bend is a child in a heap, face sidewalk scraped, she's been trampled by work-boots an horse hooves. Then's when on a sudden 'Go turns to me, urgent, must be he saw somethin I didn't see.* "Kit 'lady"—*he snatches me up so my feet leave the ground—* "Sweetness, I've loved you; I meant to get straight—" *Then comes what cuts through the sound like a cannon . . . a huge loomin flare . . . an there's nothin but air,* there's not need to care! *an in darkness I see a woman who's me tryin to smile for an eternal while.*

I couldn't help but light into Lena, the Kitty in me, she had to come through. "It was you who made 'Go go through what he did."

"You might want to consider doing something for your-self instead of doing for 'Go," she said, nervy, pale as could be, with that push-bossy 'tude I could see through the cracks in 'Go's recall of his fast-movin mother. It's a good thing she caught me at this phase of daze, damnear nappin. "Meanin what?" I flipped at this thing, whatever she must be, haint or early nightmare, gate-crashin late day.

Dampness and chill filled the air. "Seems to me you're

beating a dead horse, and you're thinking deep down that
you are."

"'Go's a dead horse to your eyes?"

"Chicago's my son, now that's a fact, but does what's
cut-and-dry have to limit my eyesight?"

"Depends on what you wanna see."

"What's there to be seen? That's what I want to
see."

"You tellin me to give up on your son?"

"I'm telling you to start up on yourself. You can't
remake a man—"

"What kinda thing is that for a mother to say? You
be soundin unnatural."

"An you be soundin hardheaded as hell all froze over."
The girl had stiffened when she mocked her, so she
smoothed her way through the rest. "I said all that to say
this." Mist-covered notes flowed toward the girl. "It's a
curious thing; most women think we can make our men
over, maybe because we made them that first time at their
birth, we fall prey to pride, womb-ego maybe; we just don't
know when to stop." Her migrant facility guided her back,
through illusive cities of plains. "Lord knows I missed my
own prompts time and again, I couldn't seem to recognize
the signs all around me, all of them reading *Detour
Ahead.* . . ."

"You gotta break that on down. Some a us ain't as
high-flown as you in our savvy."

Patience untacked its grip from reasonable mien. The
youngster had spunk that she'd need, but what she should
do now was shut up and listen to menopause-truth laid out
before her, pre-bled and earned by her forebears in feeling.

The youth of today, they have to be heard, lest you think they have more sense than they do. . . .

"What beats me," the girl let her know, "is how you manage to set yourself aside from 'Go like the two of you ain't even blackblood connected."

Blood has its limits. The image of blood was a wash of bled hope; blood was a little-known network of cell-to-cell linkage where each molecule had to spin in its place on its own. "All right then, you tell me. Just what are you doing for you?"

The girl waited a moment, looking at mobilized air through down-slanted scant-belief eyes. Rawness rared up about the young woman and showed what it meant: pitch and bulk courage, grit unsifted down, at the ready. Would that 'Go had what Lena's lambency felt in the girl. Yet the girl seemed so lacking and fretful, as if she were waiting for rescue. In manifest life Lena's temper'd been short for such fill-in-blank women; they seemed not to know their own minds til life ground them down to do-or-die level where they found themselves pulverized into potential.

" 'Go, he's so fulla the blues," Kit was saying. "He's got blues all locked in his soul."

The impression of warning inched forward on gargoyles' clawed paws. Yet Kit looked to cipher the suggested elder so near her. 'Go's mother had been in her fifties and from what 'Go had told her, she'd always seemed distant, removed, in no need of approval, leastwise from outside the bounds of herself. "I knew Chicago as downright as anyone know him," the girl stated flatly. "I'd venture to say I cared for him too, least much as you."

Occasion took stock of taut time in its tempo, including the slip of a girl with her apparent daring, spine afterall, disguised as uncouth. "You got somethin to say? Go 'head then an say it," Kit said to the presence there in the room. "I'm one for straight talk, no fancified dancin with big empty words; that ain't my line an I thank God it ain't. I may seem green to you, or unready, but I'll tell you one thing. I know the score about you." 'Go had pulled Kitty's coat to this mother of his, overseas mistress of fame an a bigtime ofay. She had her nerve, comin on strong as hincty-time queen—there's a worlda difference tween *heart* an sheer monkey nerve. One's born of ignorance; the other of verve. If it hadn't been for her in 'Go's life, he'd a likely had some sense a himself. 'Go cut his ma all the slack in the world, but she, Kitty, was unimpressed by pretension an airs. Lena had slipped into the role of a mother after her child was nigh grown an could fend for himself, or woulda been able, if not for the jinx of his birth into maternal dearth. Kit set her mind she'd ask the intruder straight out.

"If you loved him like you say, how come you ditched him when he was a kid?"

In distance there rumbled a rinky-dink tune riding blues gloom of a chanteuse's voice.

"There were things I had to do to be any good for Chicago or for myself. . . ."

"Yeah, sure, I know."

Sanction sagged for a moment. What had the visitor sought via exchange with this unexposed slip of a girl? "I don't expect you to understand."

Kit shook her off. "I pick up tips in a jiff." Once she was onto hunt grounds, she knew not to stall, just to aim for her mark and she always did, it was part of the spark that fired up her gumption folks spoke of. "When you came to 'Go's life, runnin your motherhood scam to him then when he'd run off from home an was out on his own livin on grace in a boardhouse. . . . Weren't you a mite overdue?"

The lifeforce of Lena retreated to refuge in a lone realm where deterrent wind blew barrenly through black sapless trees. When she reentered light, she'd resume with the girl.

Kitty was waiting. "You runnin off when the heat gets too warm?" She sucked her teeth briefly. "Don't let me forget; that's your way. I ain't used to that, see, not from a woman." She almost added, *like me.* "We stand our ground, where I come from . . . where I *be.*"

"So I see."

The reserved older woman seemed to mock her, to take stock of Kit's secret woes and own whims. She wanted to hush but felt her inner self rush the intruder, using a rawhide of words as her whip. " 'Go cared for you to the end, then when he said you 'died weird'. . . ."

"Go right ahead. I'll put up with you."

"Like 'Go made do without you for all a his growing-up years? That was his problem."

"I'll grant you, it may have been one."

"One like that's all you need." Kit thought of her own arid childhood, her mother stayed gone, maidin for whitefolks, mindin a whole world of younguns outside of her own. *Whenever I reached out for softness,* she told her worn dream of remembered Mama, *you pricked me with your jagged edges instead.*

Something bucked up in the trespasser meanwhile; it

stood on hind legs to get Lena's attention, then thundered
on hooves through misty awareness, the clouded fen of
recall. As a child of foregoing life, she'd damped her
dreams down and sought sheer survival through tactics she
worked on her own. *"What don't bend, it'll break in strong
wind."* She reconciled memory of mustardy Minge and her
unsettled uncles; their voices of discord rode nickelodeon
rolls she could make out as ghost ragtime notes, reintroduced through reconjured fear.

Then came the rest of the riders unbidden: Being a
pawn in *Cam's games made for your own rerouted, aberrant
aims.* . . . A voice like her own had been whispered the
thought as suggestion reharkened and sharpened on keenly
cut barbs of earlier conscience. *You had to break free of
the sickness of self that you felt.* The voice laughed a fast
hollow trill of minor-key tones. *You had to try—didn't you
now?—to make it alone on your one-minded own.* She
hadn't been able to brace and accept what she'd stooped
to in order to keep him, that self-focused man that she'd
never had— *But he fed you your music*, said the sayer.
He brought you to where you stood there that day. Where
the cabaret crowds couldn't abide what she say in the way
that she sang it.

> *. . . since you and I
> have drifted apart,
> Life doesn't mean
> a thing to me. . . .*

I let a sonnnng . . . go out of my heart— She'd sung
them her favorite tune in the cabana and reaped their lack
of attention, their studied indifference to feeling she
couldn't manage to share with those who'd come just to

feed off her pain, or was it that something inside her reserved her own best for itself. Her public's disdain? It shocked and unnerved her, til the time that she realized she'd reaped what she'd sown: unnatural neglect. Over the years spent in Montevideo, what she'd sown had grown tenfold; disdain became ripe ill-regard. She could manage to work past the jeers of the crowd until they happened to echo her own.

There was no living with Camvren for long, that was obvious when he'd begun to beckon her stand-ins no matter that she still was on the marquee. So it was that she headed back for the States when prosperity'd snapped shut the vise of its promise; the stars were against her it seemed. That was in rank '42 with its bigwigs and rash desperation gripping the bulk of the country already, then when she'd found a . . . what could she say? A "position." She didn't need her sins recounted to her; long ago she'd composed her own litany, urged it to life every day.

But the girl's voice assailed her. " 'Go told me you'd moved back to Chicago when he was fifteen."

"When I saw 'Go again, he seemed happy and said it was so," she said simply.

Kit wouldn't be slowed. "How come you didn't take him in then? You coulda gave him a hand."

From a cathouse? It was where she'd wound up and the scheme of descent still amazed her: how everything automates into place to the tune of 6/8 time despair. That's what she fell into—the hole gape where principle takes you. And wasn't it true? She'd started by simply responding to one in the swarm of requests for her off-duty service in bodily music played in the key of degenerate senses, she'd traded herself for the discord of currency earned in a mode out of key. What brought her to it? Need, and a greed to consume what was left of her unsuited self.

When she centered again on the girl, Kit was looking in Lena's direction with stark upraised eyes. "What've you got to say for yourself?" the girl asked intransigently.

'Go would come to understand, she'd told herself. He'd seemed strong when she reintroduced herself, and able to learn apt lessons of life on his own.

"He knew what you did," the girl told her. "You threw him to Meech 'steada straight to the wolves."

Chicago would understand later. So her suicide wasn't offense or malfeasance; it had been hope of redemption for what she had done because life is a song that scourges your sins from around you and clears passage to heaven, or down toward the hell of our birth on this earth.

> *It was the sweet-test mel-o-dy. . . .*
> *I know I lost heav-ven . . .*
> *'Cause you were the song.*
> *Since you and I*
> *have drifted apart,*
> *Life doesn't mean*
> *a thing to me . . .*
> *Please come back, sweet music,*
> *I know I was wrong.*

On the bridge of her song Lena was gone, leaving me up from my foregoing doldrums, ready for new times of Welcome! to Plexus, digging what I had to do. The moment I posed fingers on keys of proud Plexus, I started to real-eyes that rhythm's the glimmer that sparkles the motion of me in my ecstasy, free; and piano's percussion all the way through. The stirrings within me demanded fidelity; I would see if I can manage to come from within, to come up to snuff, work my stuff on the stand of my muse-echo stage . . . . And if my muse-ic didn't come through, I knew what to do: Let my foresister Kit, alternative me in my own fantasy— Just let my Kitty come through!